DEADLY CARGO

MYDWORTH MYSTERIES #5

Neil Richards • Matthew Costello

RED DOG

UK

Published by RED DOG PRESS 2020

Originally published as an eBook edition by Bastei Lübbe AG, Cologne, Germany, 2020.

Edited by Eleanor Abraham
Cover Design by Oliver Smyth

ISBN 978-1-913331-14-6

www.reddogpress.co.uk

1.

TROUBLE ON THE ROAD

BARRY HOBBS WAS driving his lorry slowly – carefully – the six-cylinder, four-ton vehicle comfortably eating up the miles, its twin headlights lighting up the tarmac road ahead.

Emblazoned on the side were the words of the company he worked for: *Excelsior Radios*. And inside, as he knew only too well, securely stacked in wooden crates, his precious and delicate cargo.

Eight Windsor radio phonographs. Top of the Excelsior range. Walnut finish. Built-in speaker. Valve radio.

The very best of British engineering. And each one worth every penny of its fifty-guinea price tag.

If you had money to burn, of course.

Which Barry certainly didn't. Not on his wages.

The lorry could usually manage a faster speed, especially on a main road like this, but – though Barry would have preferred to do this delivery run to Manchester as fast as possible – this time he was staying *alert*.

Looking for signs of anything wrong, anything that should cause him alarm, his hands tightly gripped on the large steering wheel.

He looked across the cab, out of the passenger window. To the west, the sun had gone down, but there was still light in the sky. Clear blue sky, making the daylight linger.

Good, he thought. *Might catch up a few miles before it's dark.*

Though he had yelled at his mates on the loading bay to *please hurry it up*, it had still taken hours for them to get the giant radio phonographs out of the warehouse, all boxed up carefully for the journey.

Mustn't have a nick or a scratch anywhere.

Customers paid plenty for them. And those customers wanted perfection.

But the loading-bay team had moved slowly, what with it being a Monday and so many lorries heading out, and there'd been nothing Barry could do to get on the road early.

Early, well – at least before dark.

And now, like it or not, he had a good number of hours ahead of him on the road – at night. He'd only just passed Oxford – hardly half way there.

Absolutely nothing he could do about that.

And while, oh yes, there were a few shortcuts he knew – narrow Cotswold lanes that went up towards Cherringham, clipped a few minutes before they came back to the main roads – he had decided, after what happened just over a month ago…

It's strictly the main road for me.

Those shortcuts, so twisty, hedges scraping the side of the big lorry, barely fit for a car.

But in truth – it wasn't the width of those roads that gave him pause.

He took a breath, trying not to think about it.

Instead he thought of getting to Manchester. Unloading. Then, to the Bricklayer's Arms, hopefully in time for one of their greasy meat pies and a pint.

Not exactly the life, Barry thought.

But – like it or not – it was his life.

THIS MAIN ROAD seemed emptier and emptier as he snaked his way north – the occasional car, or another lorry, passing – his own headlights now properly cutting the gloom.

He had a thought, with these long drives, delivering the expensive radio sets… *wouldn't it be great if the damn lorry had a wireless radio!*

Wouldn't be so bored.

Barry was thinking the same thoughts over and over.

But always, in the back of his mind, that bit of fear.

And when he had that worrisome thought, he told himself, *Cor, what are the odds?*

There's no *odds. Lightning doesn't strike in the same place twice.*

Even if it wasn't exactly "lightning" he was thinking about.

He thought of his wife, Molly. Their two little 'uns, Sam and Ellie, whom he loved to bits.

Thinking of them, always gave him an added boost when he was midway on his trip.

Midway. *Halfway.*

Sometimes Barry Hobbs spoke out loud to himself, saying, "Almost there! I've got this covered, I have."

Even as he passed little side roads that he knew were shortcuts.

Shortcuts he didn't take.

AFTER ANOTHER THIRTY minutes had passed, he saw something ahead, barely picked up by his headlights.

Something blocking the road. And as Barry slowed (while his heart picked up its pace), he saw it was a tree trunk.

He could see a car, headlights on, on the other side of the felled tree. Someone standing beside the trunk. Black car, man in a hat. A fedora.

Barry slowed even more, until he brought his lorry to a full stop a few yards short of the tree.

And now he could see the man, still just a shape, looking at the tree limb barring his way, heading in the other direction.

For a second, Barry thought about getting out of the cab, jumping down, having a quick chat with the other driver, as you do in such situations.

But he stopped himself. Thought twice about it. *Given the circumstances.*

With a shake of the head, the man got into his car, and began making a three-point turn that actually needed an additional back and forth, before he turned around, rear lights glowing like eyes, until they and the car disappeared in the distance.

Barry looked down at the seat next to him. *The Motorist's Road Atlas of Great Britain.* Latest edition, but still not totally reliable, Hobbs knew.

This tree wasn't going anywhere tonight. He was going to have to find another route. He remembered seeing a few small roads, a half mile or so back. No question. He'd have to use one of them.

The atlas popped open to the page covering this part of the Midlands.

He grabbed his torch from the small compartment to his left. Flashed it up and down.

Yeah, he thought. *Couple of minor roads – should work.* And he used his finger, the torch's light trailing, to trace a route.

One – not too far back – looking nice and straight for a bit, a Roman road for sure.

Them Romans did a good job when they invaded!

But then he could see it turned twisty before it joined what looked like another main road that Barry knew would get him to Birmingham and then Manchester.

He checked his side mirrors and slammed the gear into reverse.

Licked his lips.

No one behind him. That was a good thing. For a lot of reasons.

He now had to do so many back-and-forths with the big lorry, gears crunching, to finally get it facing in the other direction.

Lost some valuable time here, he thought, finally ready to move on. And that Roman road was going to be a sizeable diversion.

Already he was seeing that meat pie and pint, fading away.

And that's not all I've got to worry about, he thought.

THE STRAIGHT SECTION of Roman road was firm and true, but then it ended in the usual series of twists and turns that made up most of England's roads.

Barry had to drop down through the gears and go slowly, the Excelsior lorry not really fit for such a snakelike path around fields and streams and woods.

All the while, not a single car came the other way. Which was a blessing.

But also – perhaps puzzling? Had nobody else been forced to come through this way?

Nobody at all?

"Blimey," he said, his hands locked on the steering wheel, the engine straining with the constant gear changes. "Come on old girl, you can do it."

He knew it couldn't be long now before he rejoined the main road.

Yeah, get back on the proper route, and away we go. Maybe a little more foot on the throttle. Make up some time.

But when he turned round one last tight bend, hedgerows brushing both sides of the lorry, he saw, dead ahead, a dark shape.

Barry quickly went to the brake, gently pumping it. Stopping short on a bend like this? Damn lorry could go head-over-heels.

Lights came on and he saw another lorry, facing this way.

Men outside, the back of the lorry clearly open.

Barry gulped. He felt himself begin to sweat, even as his braking brought him to a full stop.

And he thought, *God, not* again...

BARRY STAYED IN his seat, as two men came over. They had caps on, pulled down tight. Faces looking like they'd been smeared with some oily smudge.

No way in hell they could be recognised... or identified.

Each man had a shotgun. As one came to the driver's side, the other went to the passenger side.

More shadowy men in black woollen balaclava hats, their faces completely concealed, stood nearby.

A team, Barry thought.

Just like last time.

The man at his door climbed up to the lorry's running board, popped open the door, pointed the barrel of the gun at Barry's head...

And spoke.

His voice low, gravelly, as if he was making an effort to change it.

The words, short, clear – and reinforced by a movement of the gun.

"Get out. On the ground. Hands behind your head."

BARRY SAT ON a rough patch of ground, the hedge behind him. He watched the crew unload the Excelsior truck, and carry the well-protected radios to the other truck.

So fast!

If they ever needed another line of work, a team like this would be great working the loading dock.

But then, they *had* to be fast. Somehow they'd shut this road off so that no one would come through. Maybe another tree limb, a pretend broken-down car?

Barry could imagine these blokes must have thought of everything, as he watched the last massive radio carefully fitted into the other truck.

And that truck, nothing special about it, nothing you'd remember. Black, beaten up. Licence plates muddy, unreadable.

For now, Barry guessed.

The man who had told him what to do walked over. He pulled out a revolver from a back pocket, and tapped Barry on the top of his head with the barrel.

Hard enough to cause pain.

"You. Sit here. Fifteen... twenty minutes. Don't even *think* of moving before that."

With the gun barrel still resting on his head, Barry nodded.

The man grunted, and then with one more tap, turned, and walked back to the loaded lorry, engine already running, lights thrown on... then climbed up to the passenger seat, the rest of the crew in the back with the radios.

Barry's hands remained locked behind his head as he watched the lorry spit out a heavy cough of exhaust, then begin to chug away.

Lightning does strike twice, thought Barry.

How unlucky can one bloke get?

How am I going to tell when fifteen minutes has gone by? What if someone's watching me?

So, he sat there, in the dark, under the stars, rocks digging into his backside, the night turned cool.

Knowing that when the time was finally up, there'd be only one thing to do...

Drive all the way back to the Excelsior factory.

And wouldn't that be fun?

2.

TEA TIME DEFERRED

SIR HARRY MORTIMER came hurrying down the stairs – a perfect day for a round of golf, planned for this afternoon with his old schoolmate, Terry Wilson, all arranged at the Royal Ashdown Club. And he had an idea.

Beautiful day like today – maybe Kat might like to make up a foursome, get Terry's wife along too?

But when Harry came into the sitting room, he heard voices.

"Um, Kat I—"

And he stopped at the entrance, the bevelled glass doors open, to see Kat on the dark blue love seat, while facing her, on the big maroon leather sofa, sat Nicola Green and another woman.

From whose crumpled expression Harry guessed that something unfortunate had occurred.

His first thought: *Kat won't be able to join us for a round at the Ashdown.*

"Oh, Harry – good, you're here. Nicola called. I said to bring Mrs Hobbs straight over."

Harry smiled, nodded. "Nicola, Mrs Hobbs."

Nicola was, Harry well knew, one of the "stars" of Mydworth. Running the hand-to-mouth Women's Voluntary Service, she was dedicated to changing the lot of women, this day, this age, *right here.*

And with Kat now working two days a week alongside her, he couldn't be more supportive.

Still, Harry had the sudden feeling that what he was about to hear might affect his afternoon plans.

He pulled an armchair close to his wife. At which point, Maggie came in with a tea service.

"Oh, Sir Harry, I didn't know *you* were joining them. We'll need another cup!"

Harry was about to tell her not to bother but, all things considered, tea might be exactly what was required, and he let her hurry off to get a cup. He turned to the others.

"So, tell me. Is there something up?"

He saw Kat's dark eyes on him. Did she guess he might be a tad disappointed, losing his round? She knew him well enough to know that his sense of duty was deeply ingrained.

"Sir Harry," Nicola started, "Mrs Hobbs came to the WVS first thing this morning."

"My husband, he doesn't know a thing. Think he'd be ashamed, don't you know?"

The woman's eyes scanned Kat and Harry too.

"Why don't you tell them what happened, Molly?" said Nicola.

Molly Hobbs nodded.

"You see, my husband works for Excelsior."

Harry leaned over to Kat, thinking – while she was still getting to know Mydworth and the surrounding area after only a few months here – she may not have heard that name.

"They make radio phonographs, Kat. Absolute top-of-the-range, so I've heard. I do believe they have a new factory and warehouse just beyond the station."

He turned to the women on the sofa. "Am I right, Mrs Hobbs?"

Mrs Hobbs nodded. "Barry, he's a *driver*, you see…"

"Your husband?" said Kat.

"That's right, my hubby," said Mrs Hobbs, as if everyone knew Barry. "Anyway, about a month back, while he was doing one of his runs, he got stopped, and his entire lorry full of radios… *taken!*"

"Really?" said Harry, leaning forward. "Didn't hear a word about that."

"That's as maybe," said Mrs Hobbs, dismissively. "Everybody knows that's not the *first* time they've lost a lorry, oh no. But they're keeping tight, they are, got a lid on it for some reason."

While Harry pondered that information, Maggie returned with an additional cup.

Harry took it and started pouring the tea. "I'll do the honours."

The steeping tea sent a small smoky plume up in the room – the morning sun illuminating the few dust motes that had escaped Maggie's diligent attention.

Kat leaned forward, her voice gentle. "They went to the police, I imagine?"

"Oh, yes. But the police didn't find nothing. Just like they didn't with the other robberies. So – everything went back to normal. Least that's all we heard about it. But then—"

Suddenly Harry thought the idea of roaming about over manicured greens chasing a white dimpled ball with a golf club wasn't half as interesting as this.

"Then, just two nights ago, it happened *again*. His whole load… taken!"

"Now *that* is bad luck," Harry said.

He noticed that Nicola had taken a cup and passed it to the woman who seemed preoccupied sharing her story.

"Well, you see m'lord—"

Harry leaned forward. "Just 'Sir Harry', Mrs Hobbs. Lowly baronet and all that."

Harry's words seemed to have the effect of loosening the tightly wound woman.

She sniffed, took a breath.

"Yes, Sir Harry, it was bad luck. And that's what my Barry thought. But then they sacked him."

"They?" said Kat. "You mean the company?"

"Well, the fella what did the firing… that transportation boss… Mr Fowler. But I'm sure he did it under orders from the owner Mr Powell."

The name was new to Harry. He certainly didn't recognise it from any town matters that he had been involved in since his return from the Middle East with Kat. And he didn't think he had seen him at any of his Aunt Lavinia's "do's".

"Well, that seems dashed unfair," he said. "Chap gets robbed on the road? Well, get mad at the robbers. Track *them* down."

The woman put down her tea cup since her hands had started shaking again. "Spot on, Sir Harry! I mean, we have two little ones. We got bills to pay – got to eat like other people. Whatever will we do now?"

Nicola reached over and patted the woman's hands, entwined together. "The Woman's Voluntary Service can see to some support, Molly. You won't go hungry."

Another sniff. And the woman turned from Nicola, to look again – eyes pleading – straight at Harry and then Kat. "But he's been with Excelsior ten *years*. Don't you see? What else does he have? He's a good man. A good father. Why should he carry the can?"

And at that, Harry felt the double-barrel look of two pairs of eyes: Kat, not needing to say a word to him, and Nicola, whose eyes maybe held a flicker of hope.

Caught in the crossfire.

And Harry nodded.

"Tell you what, Mrs Hobbs. Why don't we have a little chat with your husband—"

The woman quickly began shaking her head.

"No, no. The man has too much of that beastly pride. If he even *knew* I was here asking for help…"

Harry felt like the proverbial balloon, air suddenly released.

Kat was quick to the rescue.

"Mrs Hobbs… Molly… what if—" Harry, like the two women, hung on Kat's words, her sudden plan. "What if we drive over to the Excelsior factory. Meet with the owner, this Mr Powell. See if we can discover why on earth he fired your husband? And maybe, see if he might rethink that decision."

Yup, golf is definitely *off for today,* thought Harry.

The plan was quite direct in the way he'd come to expect of his American wife.

Molly Hobbs was quick to respond.

"Oh, would you? I mean, being the two of you are so important in Mydworth."

"Not sure about that," Harry said with an easy smile. "Maybe back in the middle ages we might have been able to round up a few knights, but these days…"

"Oh, he'll listen," said Mrs Hobbs, with what seemed like a deep understanding of the natural order of things, "I'm sure of it."

"Well. Worth a shot, as they say," Harry added, smiling.

And, at that, he saw Nicola reach out and ever so gently touch Molly's arm. "We'd better let them get on with it, Molly."

Nicola got up and guided the shaken woman out of the sitting room – not an especially grand room, being simply the Dower House – but probably far more impressive than anything Mrs Hobbs experienced on a day-to-day basis.

Harry took Kat's arm as they followed them to the door.

DEADLY CARGO

As Mrs Hobbs said her goodbyes and stepped out into the porch, Nicola turned to Harry, her voice low.

"Harry, thank you. I'm always grateful... how you'll drop anything to help."

"No guarantees," Harry said.

"See you in the office tomorrow, Nicola," said Kat.

And when their unexpected guests were gone, Harry turned to her.

But Kat was first to respond.

"Sorry about your round of golf."

"The links will still be there tomorrow."

And as they walked back into the sitting room, ready to plan their trip to the Excelsior factory, she said, "You know – if I ever forget why I married you just remind me of moments like this."

"Oh, don't worry, I *will*. In fact, I keep a little diary of such things. And let's not forget all my other redeeming attributes."

At that, Kat laughed, and came close, pressed one finger gently on his lips.

"Oh – I don't need reminding about those..."

3.

EXCELSIOR

KAT DROVE. She and Harry had worked out a system that quickly determined who got behind the steering wheel of the speedy Alvis.

Namely, whoever got there first got to drive.

Even though sometimes she could almost feel Harry's entire body tense when she took a tight curve or a single lane tunnel at speed.

"So, Kat, when we get there, any ideas?"

"Guess we just go right in and meet the boss – this chap Powell."

"Absolutely agree," said Harry, grinning. "One hundred percent."

Kat laughed. "Any suggestions how we do that? Aside from flying by the seat of our pants?"

"Oh, *that* never did me any harm…"

And Kat turned her attention to the road that led past the station to the outskirts of Mydworth and the brand new Excelsior factory.

It was not a road she knew.

"Should be a little lane down here on the left, if I remember correctly," said Harry, and Kat slowed down.

"Not so little," said Kat as she saw what was clearly a newly-built road coming up. A smartly painted sign indicated "Excelsior Radios – *the Sound of Quality*".

She turned in, and then hit the brakes hard.

"Look out!" cried Harry.

An enormous truck, filling the whole road, was barrelling towards them.

Kat wrenched the steering wheel and flung the car, rear sliding, almost off the road as – at the last moment, horn blaring – the truck veered left and roared past them, just inches away, and turned onto the main road without stopping.

She took a deep breath and looked across at Harry, who shook his head and gave a short whistle. A nod in the direction of the barrelling truck.

"*Someone* got out of bed the wrong side, this morning," he said. "You okay?"

"Glad we had the brakes done last week."

"Think we've got your quick reaction to thank as much as the brakes."

Kat put the car back into gear, pulled back onto the road properly, and they carried on.

A COUPLE OF minutes later, the smooth tarmac road led them up over a small rise and then down into a valley where, surrounded by groves of trees, she saw the Excelsior factory.

A low, wide building, glass-fronted, a stylish art-deco design, with the Excelsior logo emblazoned above the entrance.

"Gosh," she said, as she pulled up in the parking lot out front. "Very modern."

"Yes. And rather un-Mydworth," said Harry. "See what happens if you go away for a few years? This is Sussex after all, not Lexington Avenue in your Manhattan."

"My Manhattan? I don't exactly own the city yet…"

She saw Harry grin, and they both watched as another big truck pulled out from behind the factory and headed off down the lane they'd just driven up.

They climbed out of the car, walked up to the main factory entrance, and went in through double glass doors.

"This place… more like Detroit than deepest Sussex," said Kat, leaning into Harry as they crossed an expanse of tiled lobby – dizzyingly geometric tiles on the floor – to a reception desk, where a smartly dressed young woman sat, perched at her typewriter.

"Good morning," said Kat, smiling. "We have an appointment to see Mr Powell."

"Certainly, madam," said the woman, with a perfunctory smile back. "Just take the lift to the first floor."

"Thank you so much," said Kat, taking Harry's arm and leading him across the vast lobby to the elevator.

"Neatly done," said Harry.

"You're welcome."

"Such a natural liar you are," said Harry. "A true gift. I really should be more careful around you."

"It was a low-risk play," said Kat, pressing the button. "Big place like this, they don't keep the boss's diary out front."

"That so? Well, I live and learn," said Harry, as the lift arrived and they both stepped in.

"YOU SEE," KAT SAID to the woman at the desk, in her guardian position outside the office of *William Powell, Chief Executive* – as it said on the shiny plaque. "My husband and I were hoping to just have the briefest of words with Mr Powell."

The woman smiled. But her eyes… steely.

Kat noted she was dressed well. Beyond what one might expect, even for an Executive Secretary.

Round her neck, a simple silver necklace, a pin in her lapel of something that she could not make out. Lipstick – not the deepest of reds, but certainly in that family, perfectly applied.

No longer young, so probably someone who had been with the company for a while. And, in a word, *meticulous*.

Kat turned to look at Harry who – for now – stood at the floor-to-ceiling window, presumably checking out the layout of the rest of the factory.

"I understand. But, you see, Mr Powell has absolutely no free appointments today. I suggest you call and make a proper introduction."

The woman, besides being well put together, was clearly pretty efficient at keeping people away from the gate.

Kat looked at Harry, her eyes, with a slight roll, signalling *your turn*.

Harry nodded, then walked over to her side, and with a breath and the smallest of throat clearings said, "Um, Mrs Hollis?"

"Miss Hollis."

"Ah, my apologies. Miss Hollis, please, let me assure you, Lady Mortimer and I totally understand the situation."

And at that, Kat couldn't help but smile. The word "Lady" having more than the desired effect.

"I'm sorry", Miss Hollis said. "Lady Mortimer?"

Ball again rolling, Kat jumped in. "Yes, you see Sir Harry and I really need to have this conversation – very brief – today. So, if there was any way at all you could see if Mr Powell—"

Switch thrown, the Chief Executive's secretary (though Kat wondered if she might be more than that) stood up.

"Let me see. Such a busy schedule." A quick forced smile. Perfect white teeth. "I'll do my best."

And at that, Mary Hollis tapped on the door and slid into William Powell's office.

And Kat guessed, *This won't take long.*
One way, or the other.

IN MINUTES THEY were seated opposite William Powell.

He had the look of a man – Kat thought – who had done his share of rough work on his way up to owning this company, now managing who knows how many employees, riding the current boom of radio that had swept the nation.

"Fine factory you have here, Mr Powell," said Harry. "Quite a sizeable operation."

"Thank you," said Powell. "State of the art – them fancy architects call it. Long as it turns out my radios, that's all that matters to me."

"Gather you used to be based over Chichester way?"

"That's right. Ran out of space. My son-in-law Edgar saw the land up for sale here in Mydworth a couple of years back. Persuaded me it was time to expand. And here we are."

"Sounds like business is good."

"Can't make 'em fast enough."

"Well, what's good for you is good for the people of Mydworth, I'm sure," said Harry. "And your employees, eh?"

"Absolutely." Powell managed a smile that looked to crack the fissures on his face before saying, "So, to what do I owe the honour of your visit?"

The man's eyes narrowed behind his dark brown sea of a desk. Polished mahogany, Kat guessed. She had seen a similar item once in the British embassy in Istanbul. A desk big enough to play ping-pong on.

In fact, she thought, smiling to herself, *didn't Harry and I do exactly that once that interminable party was over?*

Oh no – that wasn't ping-pong…

She looked across at her husband. He'd gone for the man-to-man approach, leaning forward, in that confidential way he had.

"Just this, Mr Powell. Chap we know in Mydworth. A driver for you. Or rather he *was*. It seems he has, for some reason, been sacked."

Powell sniffed, snorted. "Hobbs?"

"Yes – that's the fellow."

"Came to you for help, did he?"

Kat took the baton.

"No. Not at all. His wife went to the Women's Voluntary Service—"

"Oh, *that* lot."

"—to ask for help. Confused, I guess. Scared too, Mr Powell. Two kids… and now her husband's wages cut off."

"Far as I know we gave him a bit of severance. Though by rights we didn't have to."

"Yes," Kat said, false smile in place. "Very generous, I'm sure. But the wife doesn't understand *why* he was fired. Nor do we."

Powell nodded at that. "Fair enough question. I'll tell you."

Those last words delivered as if a big secret was about to be revealed.

As indeed it was.

"SIX MONTHS AGO it started. One of our lorries – fully loaded – stopped. Decoyed. Hijacked! And since then – it's happened time and time again! Same bastards – has to be."

Harry noticed that the man looked like he wanted to bring his weighty fist down on the desk. "Stealing *my* radios."

"And the police?" Harry said.

"Useless. Happening all over – one minute Hampshire, next minute Birmingham. Every time a different police force investigating. Nobody talks to each other, between them all the coppers making a right pig's ear of it!"

"Pig's ear?" Kat said.

Harry leaned close. "A mess."

"Ah…"

"Nasty business," Harry said, looking back to Powell. "No clues or–?"

"Not a one. Doesn't seem to matter what we do – three, four weeks later, another robbery occurs."

Harry wondered if Kat – like him – was also feeling that though they'd come here to plead for a job, something far more interesting had just popped up?

"And Barry Hobbs?" Kat said, bringing the conversation full circle.

"Well, that's just it! Hobbs's truck was robbed a few weeks ago, then again just two damn days ago – oh, sorry, m'lady."

Kat smiled. "No worries, Mr Powell. I'm from the Bronx. No shortage of colourful language growing up there."

And at that, Powell produced a genuine smile.

How she can work her charms, Harry thought.

"You have to understand our position. Hobbs is the only man to have been 'hit' twice. And I'm a great believer in the theory that lightning *doesn't* strike twice. Couldn't let him stay on the payroll, let alone continue driving."

"So – you think whoever's responsible for these thefts has someone on the inside?" said Harry.

"Stands to reason, doesn't it? How else would they know exactly when and where the lorries were going to be on the road?"

Harry caught Kat's eye. Perhaps wondering if he was going to try to move this man – who, with his wealth and success, could also clearly be quite obdurate.

But he knew she would have a much better chance – and gave her the tiniest of nods.

So Kat, with her own warm smile, acted as if she had just come up with an idea.

While Harry knew well – *that idea* had probably been percolating from the moment they'd walked into the office.

"MR POWELL, I HAVE a thought. And I think perhaps Sir Harry here will find it interesting as well."

Kat saw Powell's eyes flick across to Harry then back to rest on her.

"Go on."

"Can we ask that you hold off firing Hobbs for a bit?"

"What?" said Powell, his voice rising. "You mean let him drive again?"

"No, not drive. I understand entirely why you can't allow that."

"Well, what exactly *do* you mean, Lady Mortimer?"

"What I'm asking – I think what we both would ask – is for you to delay any formal dismissal of Mr Hobbs until…" Kat looked at Harry. Was he going to be good with her next words? "Until *we've* investigated these robberies."

From Powell's expression, he hadn't expected that at all.

"What? The two of you?"

"Yes," said Kat, leaning forward, serious.

"But this is in the hands of the police. What qualifies you to do their job for them?"

Harry interjected. "Ah well, you see my wife and I, until recently, were both in our countries' foreign service. Did rather a lot of this sort of thing."

Kat could see Powell absorbing this unexpected information.

"Wait a minute," he said. "You mean you two – the pair of you – used to be some kind of... *spies*?"

Kat laughed. "Dear me, no. Not at all, Mr Powell. What a thought! No, what Sir Harry means is we used to work occasionally on... investigations for our various embassies. All very discreet, of course. 'Hush-hush', I think is the term."

"Over the years," added Harry. "In various ports of call."

"I see," said Powell. "*Investigations.*"

"Fraud," said Kat. "Theft. Delicate diplomatic issues and so on. Assisting the local police."

"Is that a fact?"

"And since we've returned to England, we have had one or two, um, successes in similar, more *domestic*, situations," said Harry. "So it's quite possible we can find out what's going on with these robberies."

Kat hurried with, "So, what do you say, Mr Powell? Let us look into the disappearance of your radios, while we tell Barry and his wife... all may not be lost yet."

"At what cost – to me?" said Powell, his eyes narrow.

"No more than a donation to the WVS," said Kat quickly.

Powell frowned as he thought this over, his face revealing again his distaste for the organisation.

"All right," he said after a few seconds. "You have a *deal.*"

Kat glanced at Harry – a small smile of relief.

"I'm so glad, Mr Powell. You won't regret it."

"I hope not," said Powell. "I assume you'll be starting right away?"

Kat looked at Harry again and he nodded.

"You'll want to look around the factory, I imagine," said Powell. "Anything else?"

"Employment files would be useful," said Harry.

"See if you can find the bad apple, eh?" said Powell. "Don't see why not. I'll get Mary to pull out the files, have them ready for you this afternoon."

"We'll need to talk to some of the staff, too," said Kat.

"That can be arranged. But first, if you can spare a few minutes, I want to show you why your 'intervention', right now, could be important. In fact – literally – life or death for Excelsior."

Now it was Kat's turn to be surprised – pleased that her idea had taken root, but also curious. *What rabbit was Powell about to pull out of his hat?*

Powell stood up, then walked towards a side door, past a well-supplied cart of alcohol in gleaming crystal decanters whose sparkle matched the polished metal of the cart itself.

Into a room that mostly resembled – to Kat's mind – the private meeting area of a very posh club.

At the door he turned and gestured them to follow.

"Allow me to show you Excelsior's latest and greatest radio phonograph: '*The Westminster*'!"

4.

STATE OF THE ART

HARRY FOLLOWED KAT into the small carpeted room and took in the strange space.

The walls appeared to be lined in velvet. To one side, a long leather sofa and a matching leather armchair.

Facing them, as if holding court, was, Harry assumed, the Excelsior Westminster radio phonograph.

A good four feet high, in warm rosewood that glowed in the soft lighting, finished like a piece of 18th-century furniture. The machine certainly was bigger – and grander even than Harry's Aunt Lavinia's radiogram, up at Mydworth Manor.

He watched as William Powell plugged the thing into an electric socket, then ceremoniously switched it on.

"Two minutes for the valves to warm up properly," said Powell. He gestured to the armchair. "Please – take a seat."

Harry and Kat sat, waiting expectantly.

Powell went over to the door, shut it gently, then returned to the radio, its control panel now glowing yellow. He glanced at a clock up on the wall.

"We should just catch the morning concert from the BBC in London," he said. He reached down and slowly turned up the volume knob.

An exquisite tenor voice began to fill the room; a gentle piano underscoring the haunting melody.

"Schubert," said Harry.

"'Du bist die Ruh'," said Powell.

"And if I'm not mistaken," said Harry, "that's Georg Walter singing."

"My God," said Kat. "It's beautiful. As if... as if he's here in the room singing!"

"Extraordinary," said Harry. "Even in a concert hall, I've never heard such a... I don't know, such a pure sound?"

He saw Powell beaming at them both, clearly pleased at their reaction.

"Exactly. Each note so crisp. So clear. This machine brings you not just the sound of music – but the very *soul*."

"What's the secret?" said Harry, stepping over to examine the machine more closely.

"Ah well," said Powell, "that would be telling. Let's just say the boys in our laboratory are ahead of the game."

Harry could see that Powell wasn't going to give any more away.

"If your other radios sound like this then no wonder people have been stealing them," said Kat.

"I suspect the seventy-five guinea price tag might also have something to do with it, Lady Mortimer," said Powell.

"Chap could nearly buy a car with that," said Harry.

"Indeed," said Powell. "But no car will *move* you like this. Thirty years I've been making radios and I can promise you there is no other set in the world delivers sound like—"

But before he could finish, Harry saw the door burst open and a younger man, suit, tie, sharp-looking – with a flushed face – stood there.

"Sir, we've got a problem with the—"

The man stopped the second he saw Harry and Kat.

"Edgar, please knock when I'm in the audio room!" said Powell.

"Sorry," said the young man, "I didn't realise we had visitors."

"My son-in-law, Edgar White. Sir Harry Mortimer, Lady Mortimer," said William.

Harry shook the man's hand while he went to Kat as well. Harry could sense Edgar's instant mood shift on hearing their names.

"Come to try out the Westminster, eh?" said Edgar, smiling now. "Isn't she a beauty? We can have a model delivered to the manor this very afternoon if you're keen."

"Ah, well," said Harry. "She certainly is something special, but in fact—"

William Powell stepped in to explain.

"The Mortimers aren't here to purchase a Westminster, Edgar."

"Oh? Then—"

"I've asked them to help us. Do some digging into these *damn* robberies."

"What?" said Edgar, frowning. "How so?"

"Turns out the two of them have quite a bit of experience in investigating," said William Powell.

"But surely the police—"

"The police have, so far, done beggar all if you'll pardon my French, m'lady. Wouldn't you agree, Edgar?"

"True, so far. But we have our own measures in place, sir, and it's a complicated problem."

"Speaking of problems," said William, "what did you want to tell me?"

"What?" said Edgar, clearly distracted. "Oh, nothing that won't wait."

Silence. Harry observed the father- and son-in-law facing each other – this difference of opinion clearly not something new in their relationship.

DEADLY CARGO

William turned to Harry. "I should explain. Whilst I am the Chief Executive, Edgar here is the Managing Director of the company. Nuts and bolts. Details and whatnot. So, occasionally we don't see eye to eye. But that's family businesses for you!"

Now he watched as William placed a hand on Edgar's shoulder.

"Tell you what," he said, "why don't you give our guests a little tour of the factory, so they can start their... detecting? That what you call it, Sir Harry?"

"That'll do," said Harry, smiling at the two men.

He waited for Edgar to react to Powell's instruction, the young man clearly still simmering.

"Yes. Of course. Why don't you follow me?"

He turned on his heel and led the way out.

William ushered Harry and Kat through the door after him, and followed them into the outer office, where he saw Edgar already engaged in a hushed conversation with Mary Hollis.

"Right then. I'll leave you in Edgar's capable hands," said William. "And I'll make sure Mary here has those personnel files ready for you this afternoon."

Harry noticed Mary and Edgar both look up. As William Powell turned to go, Harry saw Kat put a hand on Powell's arm.

"And Barry Hobbs?" said Kat. "For now. Still on the payroll?"

"Still on the payroll, Lady Mortimer," said Powell. And then with a smile, "Thanks to your persistence."

"Thank you," said Kat, and once again Harry saw that smile do its work.

"Right," said Edgar, joining them, a lit cigarette now in his hand, his face still unyielding. "Factory tour, as requested."

He crossed to a door in the corner of the office.

"This way, please."

Smiling at Mary Hollis, Harry and Kat followed.

THROUGH THE MAIN DOOR, Kat immediately appreciated the size of the factory.

They came to a long corridor. On one side a series of offices whose walls were half-frosted glass. On the other side a balcony running the width of the factory, which looked down onto what had to be the main production area.

Edgar marched ahead, speaking over his shoulder. "Along here – sales, marketing, payroll, accounts, filing, invoicing, orders," he said, indicating each office as they passed.

Halfway, he paused to stub out his cigarette and they joined him to turn and look out over the balcony, onto the factory floor.

"And down there – the assembly line," he said, pointing out the various sections. "Raw materials for the carcasses come in over there, then teams of joiners, carpenters, polishers do their stuff. That other side? All the technology. Delicate stuff that. Controls, valves, motors, speakers…"

Looking down to the assembly line, Kat could see at least fifty workers, mostly in matching brown coats, all intent on their individual tasks, the whole area so seriously busy.

"And over there, by those big doors – that where they put the radios all together?" she said.

"Well spotted. Final assembly," said Edgar. "And quality control. Last tests and all that. Very important."

"Far cry from your old factory in Chichester, I imagine?" said Harry.

"Indeed," said Edgar, finally appearing to thaw after their difficult start. "God-awful place that was. So crowded, more like a Victorian sweatshop than a factory."

"To this – so very modern," said Kat.

"Oh yes. We're very much a modern company, Lady Mortimer. Forget coal and steam. And steel. This – is the real future for our country. *Radio. Technology. This.*"

"How very exciting," said Harry. "Where will it all end?"

"End?" said Edgar, clearly taking Harry's comment seriously. "God, it's hardly beginning, Sir Harry. You wouldn't believe what—"

But then Kat saw him stop, as if he feared he might be saying too much.

And, as he turned to look at her, she could see a real fervour in his eyes. A passion.

And something else she couldn't quite put a finger on – something she didn't quite *trust*.

"This way," he said, heading off again.

Kat looked at Harry – had he noticed what she'd seen?

She saw him raise his eyes briefly and knew that he had.

HARRY FOLLOWED KAT and Edgar down a tiled staircase then through a door that emerged onto the factory floor.

Down here the noise levels were much louder but everywhere there was the sense of disciplined, diligent labour. The floors were clean and tidy; so unlike the roaring, chaotic factories that Harry had visited in the past, where desperately needed planes and tanks and artillery were quickly hammered together.

As Edgar rushed ahead, skirting the main production area, Harry saw that they passed a set of doors marked "No Entry – Restricted".

Harry saw the doors open and a young man came out. He had the look of a junior lab technician: white coat, safety goggles pushed back over wiry hair, holding what looked like a valve.

"Mr White!" he shouted, then rushed over. "This really won't do! Won't do *at all!*"

Harry saw Edgar stop to face the young man. He didn't look pleased at the surprise.

"Um, not the best time, Arbuthnot, I'm just showing—"

But Arbuthnot shook his head.

Clearly not one for social niceties, thought Harry.

"This latest shipment? It's dreadful! The nickel – we can't work with it! It's got to go back, we—"

"Timothy," said Edgar, giving Harry and Kat a glance, then gently shuffling the man to one side. "Just give me five minutes, won't you? Then you can explain the problem to me."

"It really won't do," said the technician, muttering, shaking his head as if he hadn't already made his point. "You can't expect me to—"

"Five minutes," said Edgar, a bit of bite in his voice, as he led the technician back to the doors. "I'll see you back here, in the lab. Just a few minutes. There's a good chap."

Harry watched the man open the doors into the lab, and he caught a glimpse of other white-coated technicians and stacks of electrical equipment before the doors quickly closed again.

Edgar returned, took out a silver cigarette case and hurriedly lit another cigarette.

Tad rattled, Harry thought.

"So sorry about that," he said. "Our Chief Research Officer. Bit of a character, if you know what I mean."

"Chief? He looks terribly young," said Kat.

"Twenty-five," said Edgar. "Got him straight from Cambridge. Man's a genius."

"And a bit highly strung?" said Harry.

"Don't get one without the other," said Edgar, forcing a smile.

Harry nodded towards the lab. "All looks rather hush-hush in there."

"Can't have people stealing our secrets," said Edgar, clearly wanting to close the subject. "Anyway, let me show you some of the finished radios—"

But before he could say any more, a man in a suit with a clipboard under one arm rushed over.

"Yes? What is it now?"

"Sorry, sir, but there's a bit of a barney on the loading bay. Think you're needed now!"

"Again?" said Edgar, shaking his head. "All right, be right with you."

He turned to Harry and Kat, as Harry now heard angry shouts coming from the far end of the factory.

"Sorry about this," he said. "I'll have to deal with it. Stay here, if you wouldn't mind. Be back *in a jiffy*."

But Harry shook his head. "Sounds like you might need a bit of help, old chap."

Edgar looked unsure whether to agree. "Appreciate it, thanks."

They all headed towards the rear of the factory as the shouting grew louder, and there came the sound of breaking glass.

5.

TROUBLE

KAT TURNED THE corner at the end of the factory floor right behind Harry and Edgar and took in the situation.

The loading bay – where half a dozen trucks were backed up, doors open, clearly waiting to be loaded – was deserted.

But to one side – crowded in front of an office with "Despatch" above its door – stood a group of twenty or so men.

An angry group were shouting, swearing, pressing and pushing towards the office door, where three men in suits stood, backed up against the windows, cornered with nowhere to go, and clearly shaken and frightened.

One of the windows behind the men had been smashed, and jagged pieces of glass lay everywhere.

She watched as Harry and Edgar drove straight into the crowd towards the beleaguered suits, splitting the mob and pushing them to each side.

"Enough of this!" shouted Edgar. "Make way! Come on – out of the way *now!*"

Even though Kat could take care of herself when it came to a fight – courtesy of some useful training in tight spots around the world on government service – she knew that launching in here wouldn't help.

So she waited while the angry men, prodded by Edgar and Harry, backed away a few yards and the temperature cooled slightly. Then

Edgar – maybe Harry too – waited, figuring out where the power lay in this group of angry workers.

That wasn't hard to see.

One man in his forties – stocky, muscled, an old scar visible through his closely-cropped hair – was clearly the leader, the other men flanking him, providing support on both sides.

Edgar obviously knew this worker of old, squaring up to him.

"Right then, Drew. What the *hell's* going on?"

"It's bloody Fowler, sir. He won't give us the week's schedules. He's locked us out of despatch!"

Kat saw Edgar turn to one of the men in suits. Tall, thin, pencil moustache; quick eyes, flicking round the crowd.

"That right, Fowler? No schedules to the drivers?"

"Yes, sir," said Fowler. "No weekly ones given out. Only way we can keep the lorry movements confidential, sir. All routes delivered – day-to-day."

She saw Harry look over to her, as if he might be curious what Kat made of this. She also saw Edgar nod, taking his time.

"Very good, Fowler. Right, makes sense," said Edgar. He slowly turned back to Drew.

"There you are, man. *There's* your answer. No need to make this kind of fuss. It's all about protecting the shipments, eh? Think we all want to put an end to these infernal robberies, don't we?"

Kat could see Drew working hard to control his anger.

"With respect, sir, I'm afraid you don't understand."

"Oh, don't I?" said Edgar, clearly at the edge of his patience.

"The men *need* to know where they're going and for how long, sir. So, they can plan. Tell their families. They can't just pitch up and be told they're away off to Scotland or Cornwall or Wales for two nights. We got rights, and Mister Fowler here's trampling all over them!"

A ripple of support went through the crowd, the angry drivers brought back into it again. Kat even saw some fists raised.

Wouldn't take much for this to turn physical again.

"All right, all right," said Edgar. "I understand. But still, no excuse for smashing windows now is there?"

"Let us see the damn despatch board," came a shout from the crowd.

"Like we always do!" another voice yelled.

"You're treating us worse than poor bloody infantry!"

"All right, all *right*," said Edgar, raising his hands to calm the crowd again.

Kat saw Harry lean in towards Edgar, whispering a few words in his ear. The two of them exchanged a couple more words, then Edgar nodded and turned to Fowler.

"Fowler – I assume the transport schedule is written up – as usual – on the board in there?"

"Yes, sir."

"Good. Well might I suggest you get somebody to clear up that glass, put your chaps behind the counter, and then open up the damn office so these hard-working fellows can see the driving week ahead of them?"

"The routes will get out, sir," said Fowler, shaking his head. "I really must advise against it."

"Dammit, man, if they do, they do," said Edgar.

Kat watched this stand-off between the two men, so surprising given the seniority of White. After a few seconds, Fowler gave ground.

"As you wish," he said with a shrug.

"That mean things are back to normal?" said Drew, still maintaining a bit of a snarl, Kat saw, though clearly winning this skirmish.

"Yes, Drew, they do," said Edgar.

A muted cheer went through the crowd.

DEADLY CARGO

"In the meantime, I expect to see the money for that broken window on my desk within the hour. Understand?"

"Yes, sir," came the grudging reply, as the crowd began to disperse. "We have it in the driver's fund. Least it got your attention."

Kat saw Edgar turn back to Fowler.

"Meanwhile, Fowler, I have some... er... visitors here who need to have a little chat with you. Your office in five minutes?"

"Sir," said Fowler. "As you wish."

As Fowler's men began to open up the despatch office and clear away the glass, Edgar led Harry and Kat to another office beside it, marked "Transport Manager".

As they waited for Fowler, Kat saw Edgar light up yet another cigarette. Having a rough day.

He gave a thin smile.

"Appreciate your advice back there, old man," he said. "Could have turned nasty. Needed all of us to keep a cool head."

"Easier to deal with Fowler's hurt pride later than face down an angry mob now," said Harry.

"Voice of experience?" said Edgar.

"Something like that," said Harry, catching Kat's eye.

Kat remembered the last time Harry had faced down a mob, in a small town in Egypt: a hundred-strong and armed to the teeth.

Harry took an armed mob in his stride.

If he could calm that *down,* this *was nothing.*

"Yes, so I do hope you'll forgive me for being a little unenthusiastic earlier when I heard you were getting involved."

"Quite understandable, Mr White," said Kat. "Your hands full. Doubt we looked like we'd be of much help."

"Yes. And well, my father-in-law sometimes finds it difficult to understand that he's not *really* running the show any more."

"Of course," said Harry. "Always difficult. And in these circumstances even more so, I imagine."

"Exactly. I've been doing my best to stop these robberies, but... Anyway, time has come perhaps to have some help. Appreciate it."

Kat felt that Edgar's apology was genuine. But still... something in his manner didn't ring true. Was his father-in-law's meddling really the problem?

Or was there another reason he didn't want outsiders getting involved in Excelsior?

WHEN FOWLER ENTERED the office a few minutes later, Edgar made the introductions then had to apologise as he was called away, yet again, for another urgent meeting.

"I'm sure Fowler here can answer all your questions on the robberies," he said. "Isn't that right, Fowler?"

"If you say so, sir," said Fowler. "At least as much as we know." Harry watched him take his seat at the desk.

"Jolly good," said Edgar. "Drop by the office when you're done here, I'll make sure Miss Hollis has those files ready for you. She's very efficient."

Harry noticed a quick look between Edgar and Fowler – something exchanged in that look for sure. *But what?*

Edgar nodded at both of them, then Harry watched him go, shutting the office door behind him. He took a seat next to Kat, then flipped out his notebook and smiled at Fowler.

"Quite a morning, it would seem, Mr Fowler," he said.

"Tell me about it," said Fowler, leaning back in his chair and putting his hands behind his head.

"I imagine the truck that nearly drove us off the road as we arrived was one of your disgruntled drivers?"

"Law unto themselves some of them. Especially when they aren't happy."

"Understandable that they need to know if they're going to be away from their families," said Kat. "And maybe scared too? Not knowing when they might be stopped... robbed...?"

"Maybe, yes. But I'll tell you, Lady Mortimer, I'm not convinced that one of *them* isn't behind these robberies."

"How so?" said Harry.

He saw Fowler lean forward. "I don't know how much they've told you upstairs..."

"Not a lot," said Kat. "No real details."

"Right. We were rather hoping you would fill us in on those," said Harry.

"As I said, we don't know a lot," said Fowler.

"But you *are* in charge of despatch, that right?" said Harry.

"You got it, Sir Harry. My 'domain', as it were. Every truck. Every consignment. From loading bay to customer."

"And I'm guessing the job of dealing with these robberies has landed on your shoulders?"

"True that! I'm the one knows the system," said Fowler with a shrug. "Fact – I set it up."

"That right?" said Harry. "Must be quite something."

Bit of flattery always pays off, thought Harry. *So now we know who knows what.*

"Trying to be on top of every incident then?" he continued.

As if in answer, Fowler got up, and opened a side door into a small office where a trio of assistants sat at desks, typing away.

"Got the maps in here," he said. "And the logs."

He looked at Kat and Harry and smiled.

"Want to see how it's all done?" The man grinned. "Good job you brought that notebook, Sir Harry. You'll need it."

6.

THE INVESTIGATION BEGINS

HARRY WATCHED FOWLER as he stood in front of the big standing map of Britain, like a schoolteacher in a geography class. He pointed to a small sticker on the map.

"The first robbery took place right here... in Suffolk, back in March. The lorry was heading to Ipswich, loaded with fifteen Winchesters—"

"Which are?" said Kat.

"Which *were* – then – our top-of-the-range model. Sixty guineas each in the shops."

Harry whistled. "So – nearly a thousand-pound loss. You're insured, I imagine."

"Of course," said Fowler. "And they paid out pretty promptly. First time, anyway."

"And since then?" said Harry.

"No such luck. Payments all on hold while the insurers work out exactly what's happening. If it's something happening within the company, that insurance is – as they have told us – null and void."

Interesting, thought Harry. *If Powell was involved in some kind of insurance scam – it wasn't paying off. At least – not yet.*

"What can you tell us about that first robbery?" said Kat.

"It was a night run. Nothing unusual for nearly the whole trip apparently. Then a diversion sign in the road. Came out of nowhere.

Driver obeyed it. Turned off. Followed a couple more signs and ended up in a dead end on an abandoned farm. As he got out of the cab, he was hit on the head, knocked unconscious. When he came round, the truck was gone."

"No clues at the scene?" said Kat.

"Suffolk police found tyre tracks. Couple of cars. Some cigarette butts, signs of a fire."

"They'd been waiting?"

"That's what it looked like. All neatly planned out, to my way of thinking."

"And the diversion signs?"

"Not a sign of them. Guess they all got scooped up and taken."

"What about the lorry?"

"Turned up a day later outside an abandoned factory in Reading."

"Let me guess," said Harry. "The inside, clean as a whistle?"

"Got it in one."

"You talked to the driver?"

"Of course. But he didn't know a thing, except that he got banged on the head."

"You believed him?"

"No reason not to."

"Okay. What about the next one?" said Kat.

Harry watched Fowler turn back to the map, point to a sticker on the opposite side of the country.

"One month later. Ross-on-Wye, Hereford route. Same thing. Middle of the night. Diversion. Farm in the middle of nowhere. Wallop on the head. Load gone."

"Truck too?" said Kat.

"No. This time they left the truck."

"Interesting. Let me guess," said Harry. "Truck tyre marks everywhere?"

"Correct."

"They used some of the cash from the first robbery to purchase a truck?" said Kat.

"Yes. That's how I saw it," said Fowler. "Safer to transfer the radios to their own lorry, rather than steal ours."

"Less chance of being detected," Kat said. "Smart. Same cargo?"

"Winchesters, yes."

Harry saw her look at him. She nodded. Kat the interrogator was in her element.

"Something in that, you think?" said Kat. "Maybe stealing to order?"

"Could be. Though the way I've been thinking about it… makes more sense to steal top-of-the-range. Same risk – but more profit, right?"

"And the other robberies – same modus operandi?" said Harry.

"*Modus,* oh… *y*ou mean did they do it the same way? Right. Yes, pretty much. Always at night. Always a diversion. Always a gang. And always another lorry waiting."

"Six times?" said Kat.

"Seven, counting last week."

"And Hobbs the only driver to whom it's happened twice?" said Harry.

"Only one."

Harry got up from his seat, went up to the map and scanned it. Dates, locations, time of day – all were marked.

He had some ideas, but also couldn't wait to hear what Kat made of all of this.

"Mr Fowler, think you can you send us all these details? Everything you have: reports, your notes, what the drivers said?"

"Don't see why not," said Fowler, with a shrug. "If that's what the boss wants, that's what the boss gets."

"And might be a good idea that we talk to the drivers too," said Kat. "All of them, not just the ones who've been robbed."

"Well, that there'll take a bit of organising," said Fowler, and Harry could see his supply of friendliness beginning to run low. "I mean, they're all still working. And you've seen how, er, helpful they can be."

"A problem then?" said Kat.

"Imagine the way they'll see it, is that you two are just going over the same ground as the police," said Fowler. "Not a very patient lot."

"Maybe tell them we think the police might have missed something," said Kat.

Fowler didn't answer. But Harry could see the Transport Manager wasn't persuaded.

Time to cut and run, he thought.

"Would be wonderful anyway if you could arrange it," he said. "Let them know we'll want to talk to them, at least. And thanks so much for your help today. Very useful."

And while Harry and Kat now knew a bit more, still... they didn't have much to help their investigation.

Nary a real clue in sight.

He picked up his hat, and turned to Kat. "Time we were on our way?"

Kat got up. "Yes. My thanks as well, Mr Fowler. You've given us *a lot* to think about."

Curious that, thought Harry. *Did she say those words to rattle Fowler a bit?*

Harry also reached out, shook the man's hand. Fowler's quick shake seemed to show that he was relieved to have them out from under his feet.

But at the door, Harry turned.

"Oh – just one last thing, Mr Fowler, if you don't mind."

"Yes?"

"When did *you* join the company?"

"What? Excelsior? Oh, er, February. Yes, beginning of February."

"And the first robbery was when? In March?"

Long pause.

He didn't see that coming, thought Harry.

"That's right."

"Excellent, thank you," said Harry, popping his hat on his head. "Just wanted to make sure we've got our dates lined up."

He held open the door for Kat, and with a tip of the hat to Fowler – who stood, looking confused – they left.

KAT CARRIED HER half pint of mild down to a table by the edge of the small, winding river, where a worn picnic table sat under a thick oak tree, the area completely shaded.

The nearby pub, the Tickled Trout Inn, sat behind them, the centuries-old stone building overlooking the ancient bridge that crossed the river.

Inside, locals gathered at lunch, which seemed to be mostly of the liquid variety.

Harry followed behind Kat, with his own beer as well as a plate holding some kind of sandwich he'd ordered.

She turned back to him.

"This do?" Kat said.

"Absolutely *perfect*. All on our own, for a proper little catch-up."

Kat sat down facing the river, babbling quite wonderfully in its near picture-book setting.

Nothing like this in the Bronx, she thought.

Not with all the apartment buildings and homes that had taken over the borough, complete with giant roads like the eight-lane Grand Concourse.

No such thoroughfares here, she thought.

And at times, she missed that.

Home – no matter where you go, how happy you are – always remained home.

Harry sat beside her and she looked at his sandwich, the bread hewn rather than sliced, a slab of unidentifiable meat roughly inserted.

"What actually is that *thing?*"

"Gammon, I think. Like a cured bit of ham. Looks like they chucked in half a jar of mustard too." Harry picked up one slice of bread as if opening a secret chest. "Greens of some kind. Watercress perhaps? Anyway, big enough for us to share."

He tore the sandwich in half – and let her choose which.

"You are *too* kind," she said.

"Aren't I? Cheers."

Harry raised his glass, and then Kat brought hers up for a clink. The beer, on the warm side. Would never have passed back in her father's bar. Working men – there at least – demanded an icy cold beer.

He took a sip then grinned. "Must say, you do look rather stunning in this setting, the shade from the tree, light reflecting off the river. *Fetching.*"

"Oh really? *That* word, least in my part of the world, is reserved for Fido chasing a rubber ball."

"Now *there's* an image."

He picked up his half of the enormous sandwich and started to eat. Mouth full, he said, "Okay, Lady Mortimer." He pulled out his notebook, flipped it open. "Ready for your thoughts, observations, questions... and hopefully some plans."

She picked up her sandwich, giving it a wary look as she took a bite.

"Oh, yes. Got all of those, Sir Harry."

"FIRST OF ALL," said Kat, "in my opinion, this is no amateur operation."

"I agree," said Harry. "The gang is well-organised. Probably experienced."

"And not afraid to use violence when they need to. Maybe ex-military?"

"Very possibly. Certainly sound disciplined. I'd be surprised if Scotland Yard haven't come across these chaps before now."

"Good reason for visiting Sergeant Timms?"

"*If* he'll tell us anything," said Harry. "If not, I can call in a few favours at the office."

Kat knew that Harry's work in a small and discreet department at the Foreign Office, involved liaising with various police and security services.

Which definitely had advantages when they were looking into something criminal.

"So, second thing," said Kat, "there must be somebody working for the bad guys on the inside, yes?"

"Agree again," said Harry. "You can't set up diversions, recces, hide-outs unless you have up-to-the-minute timings for the shipments."

"So – we're looking for someone who's got day-to-day access to the schedules," said Kat. "Has to be good at hiding their tracks, too."

"Someone cool, clever, calm," said Harry. "And greedy. Candidates?"

"Can't say we met anyone like that this morning," said Kat.

"Hard to tell," said Harry. "Could easily miss a suspect. Whole place was on edge. People at each other's throats."

"Can't blame them," said Kat. "Lot of jobs on the line if the company goes bust."

"Lot of money at stake too."

"Surprising though that there didn't seem to be much enthusiasm about our involvement."

"Right. Noted that myself," said Harry, taking another bite of his sandwich. "Two people, in particular. Edgar, for starters."

"Not happy at all, was he? Maybe because he's really running the show. Think our presence embarrasses him?"

"That's one theory," Harry said. "And the other person less than joyful having us aboard... Mr Fowler. The actual gent who sets up all the schedules."

"Though he did share what he knew pretty willingly."

"True. On the other hand – these robberies started soon after he arrived at the company. Coincidence? Seems doubtful."

"You think he's holding something back?" said Kat. "Hiding something?"

"Yes. Though, I can't quite put my finger on it. Also – I picked up something between him and Edgar. More than mutual dislike. You spot that?"

"I did. Least on Edgar's part. Kind of... shiftiness? Had some other thoughts too..."

Kat took a sip of her beer before carrying on.

"When we bumped into that agitated guy in the lab coat – Arbuthnot – Edgar went totally on the defensive."

"Exactly. Definitely didn't want to talk about the laboratory, did he?"

"But – well, then he positively lit up discussing the future... technology. You'd think he'd be proud of what they were doing in there, keen to show it off to us. No?"

46

"But he wasn't. Not in the slightest. Though how would that connect with radio robberies?"

She grinned at that. "Has a nice ring to it."

"What does?"

"'Radio Robberies'. Make a great radio crime show."

Harry laughed.

Kat took another bite of her sandwich and a sip of beer, the scents of the warm afternoon garden now making her feel almost light-headed.

"So," said Harry, "you hinted you might have some plans, detective?"

"Ah yes. Well, there's definitely some people we need talk to. That bullish leader of the drivers, for example."

Harry nodded and wrote that down in his notebook. "Missed that. Good catch."

Kat waited, then said, "We have other witnesses too – other drivers. Some of them knocked out – or at least saying they were. But maybe others, like Barry, actually seeing how it was done."

"*Definitely* need a chat with him. Might stir his memory if we dig deeper."

"And Arbuthnot? Gotta say… he seemed a little – dunno – *intense*?"

"That the word?" Harry said, laughing. He paused, as if almost reluctant to continue.

"There is another take on this, you know?" he said.

"There is?"

"Remember what Edgar said about that room? Top secret?"

"Oh, wait a minute," said Kat, suddenly realising what Harry was suggesting. "You mean—?"

"We know these robberies are highly organised," said Harry. "Valve technology, aerials, communications – all of that stuff would certainly interest the military."

"Got it. You think it's possible that Excelsior might have attracted the interest of a foreign power?"

Harry shrugged. "Would maybe explain why none of the stolen radios have come onto the market."

"Stripped down for the parts you mean?"

"It's possible."

"You're right. It is. In which case – dear husband – we'd best be careful."

"Right. Think I'll pop my old Colt 45 under the seat of the Alvis tonight."

"An ounce of prevention…" said Kat, always feeling safer on a case with Harry's old service weapon to hand.

The same model of semi-automatic she herself had had occasional cause to carry on government service in Egypt.

A small but effective handgun.

"Jolly good," said Harry. "Now things are getting exciting!" He rubbed his hands together. "So – what's our schedule for this afternoon?"

He squinted in the brilliant sun. She loved how he seemed so eager when she came up with a plan.

As if all this was a game.

And she guessed for them it was, even though there were thousands of pounds at stake, and possibly the future of the Excelsior company.

"Go on," Harry said.

"I want to look at those employment files, back at the factory. See who might have a grudge, new arrivals, people with a murky past perhaps. Have a chat with Mary Hollis too."

"The Ice Maiden. Think she might know something?"

"Got a feeling not much passes her by."

"Good luck with that. Meanwhile, why don't I pop up to the police station, enliven Sergeant Timms's afternoon?"

"Barry Hobbs too? Sweeten the chat with the news he's still on the payroll?"

"Excellent idea."

"By then, some of the trucks should be back. Chance to talk to the drivers."

She saw Harry ponder this. "Not sure they'll hang about at the factory. I imagine, done for the day, they'll want to visit the pub for a few."

"Not hurrying back to wife and kids?"

"Ha. English lorry drivers, dear Kat? Think they'll hit the local first."

"Local? Wonder where that is."

Harry rubbed his chin. "I'd guess the Old Station. Pretty close to the factory. Nothing fancy, a real pub for hard-working men."

Kat laughed. "No women then?"

"Oh, they might have a section cordoned off for the fairer sex…"

"How enlightened."

"Mydworth not Mayfair, you know. Best I take pub duty."

Kat laughed again. "While I head home and cook your dinner?"

"What a charming old-fashioned notion," said Harry. "But no – why don't you wait for me, let's cook together."

"Deal," said Kat. "I'll go through Fowler's reports while I'm waiting."

"Lucky you," said Harry, with a wink.

At that, he finished his glass of beer, put his hand on hers.

And the two of them sat there – Kat, eyes half-closed, enjoying this moment by the river, side by side with her husband.

7.

MEET THE WORKERS

HARRY WATCHED KAT drive off, heading back to the factory, then walked across the old bridge and headed up River Lane into Mydworth.

This was absolutely one of his favourite walks, the narrow country lane hardly used any more except for visitors to the pub – overgrown on either side with hawthorn and brambles.

Be a good crop of blackberries this year, he thought. *Must bring Kat down here. Do they have blackberries in America?*

He guessed so. Amazing things, just growing wild and so tartly delicious.

TEN MINUTES LATER he climbed the small steps to Mydworth Police Station and went through the open door.

Inside, behind the counter, Harry saw the portly figure of Sergeant Timms at his desk, a mug of tea in hand, as usual, and an open copy of the *Racing Post* beside a pile of paperwork.

Surprised, Timms was quick to slide the paperwork across yesterday's racing results when he saw Harry enter.

"Sir Harry!" said Timms, stepping up to the counter.

"Timms," said Harry

"To what do I owe the pleasure, sir?"

"Tricky business, eh? Those robberies over at the Excelsior factory?" said Harry, taking off his hat – a signal that he intended to stay for a while.

"Ah," said Timms. "*Those*."

"Mr Powell's asked me to lend a hand."

"Is that right, sir?" said Timms, frowning slightly. "That'll be you and Lady Mortimer too, I take it?"

"Indeed," said Harry, knowing that Timms – a by-the-book man if there ever was one – always needed careful... *navigation*. "Thought I should pop down and tell you, old chap. Don't want to step on your toes. I'm sure you have the case well under control."

"I see."

Harry was unconvinced that Timms did indeed see.

"Wouldn't dream of getting in your way. But you know Mr Powell – jolly persuasive. Lady Mortimer and I will just tidy up a few questions he has – save you the bother – and, of course, anything at all we come up with... be on your desk in an instant."

"I see," said Timms again.

"But I was thinking... might be good if we had a few extra details, perhaps a little squint at one or two of your files?"

"The *official* files?"

Harry knew that Timms's reputation as a sleuth had risen immensely after he and Kat had got involved in a few recent high-profile cases.

With Timms happy to take the applause and the credit.

But nevertheless, this little dance had to be performed each time.

"Well," said Timms. "Can't see it doing *too much* harm, I suppose."

Harry stood back as Timms stepped forward, and raised the counter top.

"Best come on through, Sir Harry, and I'll have my constable put the kettle on."

KAT STEPPED OUT of the elevator and crossed the plush carpet to the desk where she saw Mary Hollis typing.

"Afternoon, Miss Hollis," she said. "I believe Mr Powell has left some files for me?"

The woman barely looked up, her face impassive while she finished typing, pulling out the sheet of paper, carefully separating the carbon copy, putting the two sheets into separate trays.

A little performance – this making me wait – to tell me who's boss here, thought Kat.

"He has, Lady Mortimer," said the woman eventually, getting up and walking round the desk. "They're in my office. This way, please."

Kat followed her into a small room to one side of William Powell's office, where she could see a stack of files on the desk.

Hollis nodded to the papers.

"I'm not sure if Mr Powell told you, but on no account must they leave the building. Please ask me directly if you need to see any other files. And – yes – take care that the files do not get mixed up."

"Thank you," said Kat, trying to be as pleasant as possible in the face of this blank iciness.

The good sisters at St Thomas Elementary in the Bronx ran a looser ship than this, back when they had Kat in their charge.

For now, she smiled. "I'll do my best."

She took in the room quickly – clearly Miss Hollis's small, private domain. Some bookshelves, a make-up mirror, a large appointments calendar – and on the walls a group of framed photographs.

Photos that caught Kat's attention.

She walked over to the photos: group pictures of nurses staring grimly to camera, while behind them could be seen lines of stretchers, battered wrecks of buildings, muddy fields and blasted trees.

All not unfamiliar to Kat.

"Casualty clearing station, yes?" she said, but almost to herself, the memories flooding back, the noise, the ever-present fear, the terrible, terrible flow of losses.

"Arras, 1917," said Mary Hollis, stepping closer. "You recognise it?"

Kat nodded. "I was a little farther down the line. First Harvard Medical."

"They did good work," said Hollis.

"You were a nurse?"

"Nursing sister. But truth be told, I also ended up supervising the ferrying of supplies, wounded... all the transport of a field hospital."

Kat stepped back from the photographs, turned to look at Hollis.

Nothing more to be said; both women understanding the experience they had shared, something that only women who had been there could ever comprehend.

Kat watched Hollis go to her desk, take out a cigarette case, offer it to her. She shook her head, waited as the secretary lit up, her hostility now evaporated.

"So, tell me," said Hollis, "how on earth did you end up...?

"As Lady Mortimer?" said Kat, smiling.

Hollis nodded.

"After the war I kind of fell into government service. Then diplomatic work. American embassies all over Europe. Asia. Ended up in Cairo. Met an Englishman there – fell in love. Got married and here I am."

"Quite a journey."

"And you?"

"Oh, nothing so exotic. After... You know, when it was over... I couldn't face coming home, back to everything how it was, the old ways. So I stayed in France. Picked up work. Governess in Paris. Secretary. Translator. Came back in the end, though. No falling in love for me, sadly – rather limited supply of potential husbands."

"No shortage of men here, surely? At Excelsior?" said Kat.

"True," said Hollis. "But, let's just say, I'd be looking for something... *someone*... more."

"You like working here?"

"Mr Powell's charming enough. A fair boss. Bit old-fashioned, but then, most Englishmen are, aren't they?"

Kat smiled again, feeling a little sorry for this proud woman who – it seemed – hadn't found someone to love.

"Anyway, I'll leave you to it," said Hollis, stubbing out her cigarette and going to the door. "Give me a shout if you need anything."

Kat watched her go. Turned back to the photos for a few seconds – those horrors of twelve long years ago. Still felt like yesterday.

She sat at the desk and opened the first of the employment files.
*

Harry left the police station and walked down Rosemary Lane, then cut through to Station Road where Nicola had told him Hobbs lived.

The two mugs of sweet tea, plate of digestive biscuits, and the stack of files on the robberies provided by Timms had left him full up – but none the wiser.

Though the good sergeant did have a couple of tips for the late race at Newmarket. But not being a gambler, Harry would pass on that.

Timms had expressed his personal doubt that the thefts were an inside job, preferring – with no apparent evidence – to pin the blame on ruthless London gangsters.

And indeed – the reports he showed Harry about a spate of similar robberies a couple of years back in Kent tended to back up that theory. But those chaps had been caught – and were all still locked up.

So – any similarity was more likely to be due to copycat planning.

In fact – that seemed very likely to Harry. The robberies in Kent had been not just well-executed, but at the trial the careful planning had been revealed in detail and the press had had a field day.

Almost a template for any crooks wanting to follow in their footsteps.

Back down Station Road he walked, tipping his hat to some commuters he recognised, returning early from London. He stopped at a little run of Victorian cottages, set back just a couple of yards from the busy road.

Number 39. There it was.

He stepped up to the door and knocked.

Mrs Hobbs opened it within seconds, looking rather confused to see him.

"Oh, Sir Harry, sir, I wasn't expecting you!"

"My apologies, Mrs Hobbs, for arriving unannounced. But I bring some news that I felt you – and your husband – should both hear straight away."

He watched Mrs Hobbs process this information, then – as he'd hoped – she opened the door and he stepped into a small parlour, already lit by a flickering gas lamp in the corner.

And by that light, Harry saw what he knew must be Barry Hobbs, sitting in a small armchair by a meagre fire.

A glass of something dark and amber on the small table beside him.

A few days growth of beard.

The image: the very picture of a man who has been sacked and doesn't know what to do next.

"What's this? What's going on?" said Mr Hobbs, looking from Harry to his wife.

Harry reminded himself that she hadn't told her husband about her trip to the WVS.

Time for some quick thinking, he thought.

"Mr Hobbs, please don't get up," he said. "Name's Mortimer, Sir Harry Mortimer. Mr Powell over at Excelsior has asked me and my wife – Lady Mortimer – to help him get to the bottom of these *damned* robberies."

"Has he now?" said Hobbs, clearly still unsure what was going on.

Harry full expected the next word to be… *bastard*, or something similar.

"In doing so, it's easy for us to see that the finger of suspicion has been quite unfairly pointed in your direction."

"Too right there, Sir Harry." The man snorted. "Not a damned bit of bloody evidence," he looked straight at Harry, "now was there?"

"Exactly. So I'm glad to tell you that, effective immediately, you have been reinstated in the company's employ. Back pay as well."

"What? You don't say now."

"You've got your job back, Barry!" said Mrs Hobbs. "Isn't that wonderful!"

"Well, hang on. Not quite," said Harry, quickly. "Not completely. Full pay, yes. But not confirmed that you're back driving the lorries just yet, I'm afraid. It'll be some kind of factory work until then."

"Factory work?" said Barry, clearly feeling that wasn't good enough for him.

"For now," Harry added.

"Better than nothing," said Mrs Hobbs quickly, then she turned back to Harry. "We're so very grateful to you, Sir Harry. Barry says thank you, don't you Barry?"

Harry nodded at Barry who grunted.

These lorry drivers, Harry thought. *A tough breed.*

"In the meantime, as long as I'm here," said Harry. "Wonder if I could ask you a few questions about the two robberies? If you didn't mind?"

"Questions? Didn't I already answer a load of questions for that idiot Timms?"

Harry kept his voice steady. *Odd reaction for a man who just got some good news.* "Won't take long, Mr Hobbs."

Harry glanced at Mrs Hobbs, looking for her support. She was quick to respond.

"Now do as you're told, Barry. You answer this gentleman's questions, while I put the kettle on."

"Oh – all right then," said Barry, rolling his eyes as Mrs Hobbs went into the tiny kitchen at the back of the cottage. "Do your worst."

HARRY SAT PATIENTLY making notes while Barry Hobbs recounted in detail the two robberies.

Almost *too* much detail, thought Harry, now knowing the pros and cons of every pie and pint on offer in the pubs of Manchester and Birmingham.

When Hobbs reached the end of his tale, Harry sat back, wondering what else he could ask.

So far, no clues, and not even a sign of any threads that might lead to a clue.

He closed his notebook, and drained the cup of tea Mrs Hobbs had supplied him. "Appreciate the time, Mr Hobbs. Thank you."

"That it?"

"Unless there's anything else you can tell me?"

"No. Don't think so. All I can remember."

Harry stared at Hobbs. So far, they'd just been going over old ground.

All he needed was one clue. Just one.

"Okay. Was there nothing... odd... you noticed? Doesn't matter how small. A detail. A feeling. Anything?"

Hobbs shook his head. "Was one thing. Probably not important. But..."

"Go on," said Harry, almost holding his breath.

"Well. Both times I got robbed, you see, it took them a fair old time to load the lorries. And both times, all them blokes, moving the crates – they never said a word to each other. Not a single word."

Harry leaned forward, opened his notebook again.

"Wait a minute," said Harry. "I thought you said they threatened you?"

"Oh, the fella in charge did. But the other lads, the ones doing the lifting and carrying – *they* didn't speak. Silent as the grave, they was."

"Not even a 'up here' or a 'get a move on'?"

"Nothing," said Hobbs. "Unnatural it was. Like they was ghosts. Why would they do that? Not say anything?"

I asked for "odd", and, well, this is indeed odd, Harry thought.

"Haven't a clue," said Harry. "Wait. Maybe because you might have recognised a voice? Recognised somebody from the factory?"

"Right. I never thought of that," said Hobbs, stroking his chin. "But if that was true it would mean they got a bloke on the inside, planning it all?"

"It's a theory."

"Well I never," said Hobbs. "You got a suspect?"

"No."

"You want one?"

Harry laughed, then stopped when he saw Hobbs frown. The man wasn't joking.

"All ears," said Harry.

"*Fowler*," said Hobbs. "*My* instinct? Bent as a nine-bob note, he is."

Suddenly – this chat had turned interesting.

"Go on."

"Day he started on the job, running despatch, we could all see – all the drivers – he didn't have a bloody clue what he was doing. Lied his way into that job, Fowler did, make no mistake."

"Really? I can't see Mr White being taken for a fool. Fowler must have come recommended?"

"That's as may be," said Hobbs. "And that Mr White? Well – he's no genius either. If he wasn't married to the boss's daughter, he'd be out on his ear."

"What do you mean?" said Harry. *Now we're getting somewhere.*

"Fowler's got White round his little finger, he has. And I know why." Barry Hobbs took a breath. "And how."

Harry saw him lean forward, and cast a quick glance to the tiny kitchen as if to check Mrs Hobbs was out of earshot.

"Most of the lads know too. But here's the thing, Sir Harry. You won't get me telling you. Not with me heading back there. Loose lips, eh? Or we'd be for the high jump. So – I gave you your clue. Now you'll have to work it out for yourself."

Hobbs sat back, arms folded, nodding slowly.

Harry put away his notebook – the interview clearly over.

He checked his watch. The factory would be closing up. *Time to get to the pub.*

See if a few pints might loosen some tongues, and reveal what was *really* going on at Excelsior Radios.

DEADLY CARGO

Because Barry Hobbs – at the very last minute – had certainly set him thinking.

There are secrets in that factory yet to be revealed.

8.

AN UNINVITED GUEST

KAT CLOSED THE last of the employment files, added it to the pile and sat back to consider what she'd found.

First, Brian Fowler was clearly a hard taskmaster. Many of the drivers' files were marked with warnings and records of errors or "misbehaviours". Timekeeping failures were met with wage docking, and threats of being fired. Productivity – a speedy delivery – was closely monitored.

She could see now that almost any of the drivers might be tempted to get their own back at the company by passing on delivery routes for some fast cash.

That meant at least ten – maybe up to fifteen – possible suspects.

But, Kat guessed, chief amongst them was Reggie Drew, the man she'd seen this morning standing up to Fowler in the loading bay.

Reggie's file had him marked down – in Fowler's words – as "a direct threat to the future of the company".

Another note cited his attempts to unionise both the drivers and the factory workers.

Who can blame him? thought Kat. *The building might be modern, and the radios cutting edge but – reading these files – the way this place treats its workers is positively nineteenth-century.*

Faced with that kind of hostility from management – could Reggie be working with the hijack gang?

Nasty stuff.

And maybe Harry would find out this evening.

Meanwhile, none of the other files had suggested any other suspects.

And nobody appeared to have had anything more than minor brushes with the law – the most common offences being drink-related. Bar fights, arguments, scuffles.

Pretty typical stuff for hard-working men.

Strangely, many of these files were marked with a small "T" on the front cover, though there was no indication what that meant.

Amongst them was Barry Hobbs's file.

Barry, it seemed, had a penchant for answering back which had got him into trouble more than once with Brian Fowler: docked pay, temporary suspensions. Barry was no stranger to trouble it seemed, at least when it came to his employer.

But there was nothing in anyone's file that suggested links to the criminal underworld.

In contrast, Brian Fowler's file itself was filled with glowing recommendations from his previous employers, a biscuit factory near Portsmouth. It seemed Fowler had revolutionised the delivery system using all kinds of "modern" methods.

Mary Hollis's own file had been interesting.

From being a part-time clerical assistant at the old factory, she had risen to her current role of Executive Secretary, having worked for a year for Edgar White.

Tucked into the folder was a set of approved business expenses for a trip to Paris the year before, representing the company at a conference for radio manufacturers, which White also attended.

And yet she was retiring at the end of the year.

Strange, thought Kat, *to leave when she's clearly valued here. Perhaps something better in the offing?*

As if on cue, she heard the secretary's voice at the door.

"The office is closing, I'm afraid, Lady Mortimer."

Kat turned to see Mary Hollis, coat already on.

"Oh, I'm sorry – I didn't see how late it had got."

"Not to worry. If you leave the files here, I'll just get them back to the personnel office."

"Of course," said Kat, standing up. "I'm finished anyway."

"Anything of interest? I do hope you find out who's responsible for this *dreadful* situation. But I can't bear to think it might be someone here. *God*. Someone we know."

"Nothing so far," said Kat. "I wonder – some of the files have a small 'T' marked on them. Do you happen to know what that means?"

"Ah – a code. 'T' for Troublemaker," said the woman, clearly not approving of the system.

"Ah."

"Mr Fowler's idea, I believe."

"He certainly brooks no nonsense, does he?"

"A great believer in discipline," said Hollis.

Kat put on her coat. To change the subject she said, "I see you're leaving next month?"

"Ah, yes," said Hollis. "I've been offered a post with a company in Paris. Senior translator." The woman seemed to relax a bit. "Quite excited. I do love Paris."

"Who doesn't?" Kat said back lightly. "And... you've been before? Business trip for the company?"

"Oh yes. Sad to leave Excelsior, of course. But it's an opportunity – at my age – I can't turn down."

"You know, I worked in Paris for a while," said Kat. "At the embassy. You'll have a ball, I'm sure."

For the first time, Kat saw Mary Hollis smile.

"I intend to," she said.

DEADLY CARGO

"Well, don't let me keep you," said Kat. "I can see myself out. And thank you again for your help."

As Hollis gathered up the files, Kat headed out of the office and made her way towards the elevator.

Harry would be in the pub for a couple of hours she imagined.

Plenty of time for a long soak in the bath before supper – and the chance to think through the day's events in peace.

While she waited for the elevator, she walked over to the glazed wall that looked down upon the factory floor, lit now just by one or two small lamps.

Through the glass she could see the place was now deserted, the machines idle, all the workers gone home for the night.

But as she watched, the door to the laboratory opened and a figure appeared, peering left and right as if nervous of being seen.

Kat stepped back from the glass into shadow.

Peering down, she saw the figure prop open the lab door and disappear inside for a second – then re-emerge pulling a small trolley, loaded with boxes.

And heading towards the loading bay.

Whatever was going on didn't have the look of official business.

Kat thought about finding the personnel office, alerting Mary Hollis. But by then, the mysterious figure might have gone.

She looked around – there must be stairs direct to the factory floor.

Yes, there they were – through a set of unmarked doors.

Down she went.

HARRY PUSHED OPEN the door of the public bar and stepped into the Station Inn. The place was already noisy, crowded, and thick with smoke.

The Station Inn was long known as a working man's pub, and though Harry recognised a couple of faces – commuters from London offices, reluctant to head home so early in the evening – most of the drinkers were men in overalls, or local farmhands and labourers.

They'd spot Harry in a minute and wonder, "What's 'e doin' here?"

Most stood at the bar in groups, though Harry noticed one man sitting alone by the door, nursing a pint, evening newspaper to hand, pipe in ashtray on the table.

He made his way to the bar and, sure enough, saw Reggie Drew at the centre of a knot of men, all pints in hand, in deep conversation.

He ordered a beer from the perfunctory bartender and – while he stood waiting for the pint to be pulled – he saw one of the men with Drew look over and clearly recognise him, tapping Drew on the arm and gesturing in Harry's direction.

Instantly the men's chatter stopped and Drew put down his pint and slowly walked over.

"Drew, isn't it?" said Harry, smiling. "Say, can I get you and your pals a drink?"

But Drew ignored the offer. "Come down here to keep an eye on us, have you?" he said. "Spy?"

"Not at all," said Harry, paying for his beer and taking a welcome first sip.

"Management – they don't drink in here. It's for the working men, you see."

"Well, isn't it lucky I'm *not* management then," said Harry, smiling.

"Yer working for management."

Harry shook his head. "No. Wrong again, Mr Drew. Not working for anybody. In fact just trying to help one of those working men – Barry Hobbs – to get his job back."

Drew seemed to pause at that. "You don't need to do any of that. We can look after Barry."

"Good," said Harry. "You can take over looking after him when he comes into work tomorrow morning."

Harry could sense this was news to Drew.

"You got him his job back?"

"To be honest, my wife did," said Harry. "Though, to be fair, he won't be driving, not until we catch whoever's responsible for the robberies."

Drew's eyes narrowed.

"Going to pin it on another driver, are you? One of us lot?"

Harry shook his head. "No. Not going to 'pin it' on anybody. But I *do* think there's somebody in the factory giving out information. Has to be."

"So why the hell are you here?"

"Look, Drew, the men respect you, that's clear. So I'm hoping you can help me figure out who it is. You or maybe one of your drivers... someone must have a good idea who's behind this."

Harry saw Drew look over his shoulder at the other men, who, though now talking again, were still keeping an eye on this unlikely meeting.

"Maybe," said Drew, turning back to Harry. "What's in it for us though?"

"Nothing that I can promise you. Except, if these robberies don't stop, Excelsior will close, and you will all be out of a job. And, these days, jobs aren't two-a-penny."

"Ha! Wonders will never cease," said Drew. "A toff who cares about jobs."

Harry paused. Lowered his voice. Fixed Drew right in the eyes.

This kind of game... you had to give as good as you got.

"Look, let me explain something. I care about the people in this town," said Harry. "I like it here. And I don't want to see *anyone* out of work."

He could see Drew taking his time before nodding.

Then, a response that Harry took for success.

"Okay – what do you want from me?"

"Ten minutes of your time."

"To talk about?"

"Amongst other things... Brian Fowler."

Drew nodded.

"That bastard."

"If you say so."

"All right. Let me sort my lads out with a drink, and we'll find a corner. And I'll tell you what I know about Brian Fowler."

KAT CREPT CAREFULLY around the edge of the shop floor, past stacks of boxes, piles of timber, metal frames, radio parts.

Barely enough light to see, but in the distance near the loading bays was the dim shape of the man she'd spotted from above, now unloading the trolley by the rear shutters.

Careful not to be seen, she moved closer, darting from cover to cover, until she was just close enough to identify the mystery figure.

He paused for a second, looked around as if he'd heard something.

Kat ducked down quick enough – but not before she'd recognised who it was.

Timothy Arbuthnot – the scientist they'd met earlier.

What was he up to?

As she watched, he pulled open a door to the rear parking lot. Straight away, a small green van reversed up to it.

Arbuthnot – still acting furtive – propped open the door, then went down the steps and opened the rear doors of the van, its engine still running.

One by one, Arbuthnot picked up the boxes, took them outside and placed them carefully in the back of the van.

He shut the van doors, came back in, parked the trolley on one side, quietly slipped outside and shut the door behind him.

Through the shutters, Kat heard the van door slam, then drive away.

Somehow, she had to try to follow the van.

She raced back through the dark factory, avoiding the stacks of crates and materials.

But, as she slipped through the doors that she hoped would lead into the main ground floor reception, a sudden movement on the glazed balcony above caught her eye.

Someone stepping back quickly, out of sight, just as she had done.

Mary Hollis maybe? Here late?

But – could it have been someone else?

Her heart pounding, she went back into the deserted reception area and out through the main doors to the golden evening sunshine.

She looked across at the lane – and sure enough, there was the small green van, heading away from the factory.

Too far away to identify the driver.

She dashed across to the Alvis, hit the starter. Such an amazingly reliable vehicle, starting up in an instant.

She pulled the car round in a tight circle in the empty car park, and headed after the van.

Wondering – *if this van was involved with the robberies, was she crazy to be following it now?*

But also... shame there was no Colt under the seat.

An evening like this, she might well need it.

9.

UNDER COVER

HARRY STOOD AT the bar and ordered a second round of beers.

The pub had emptied out a bit now, but the group of Excelsior drivers in the corner were clearly settled in for the evening.

So far, he hadn't got much out of them that he didn't know already. Or that he hadn't heard from Hobbs.

The drivers in the group who'd been stopped had also noticed how the robberies took place in almost complete silence. No names, no instructions, just simple, easy to understand gestures: *"on the floor or you'll get hit"* kind of thing.

And all of the attackers had concealed their faces.

But none of the drivers believed a fellow driver could be involved. And none had a good word to say about Fowler, all with tales of the man's incompetence.

And his nastiness. Writing them up for the slightest issue.

But certainly, all of them were united behind Reggie Drew, who was open about his plans to unionise the workforce at Excelsior.

It would change everything for them.

Harry could understand that. The men were all on short-term contracts, and, like Hobbs, at the mercy of Fowler and White if they made a mistake.

Or simply got on the wrong side of management.

Drew made no effort to conceal the fact he wanted Fowler out. Maybe – Harry thought – by any means possible?

And Harry had to wonder, *how far would Drew go?*

Would he pass on information about the schedules, risk his fellow drivers' wellbeing, just to destroy Fowler?

Certainly, the man had the kind of fiery conviction that in Harry's experience went with the end justifying any means.

Harry looked up at the clock behind the bar. One more quick pint here, then time to get home, catch up with Kat.

He paid for the beers, and turned to carry the tray of pints back to the table of drivers.

But as he did, he noticed something odd.

The lone drinker, with the pipe and newspaper, had moved across the pub from the door and now sat at the table, right next to the drivers, with his back to them, newspaper still spread.

Harry couldn't put a finger on it – but there was something odd about the man.

He didn't quite belong. Yet… hanging around.

How long had he been sitting there? And why move? Either he was a slow reader, or he wasn't interested in that newspaper – because, from the look of it, he hadn't moved on from the second page since Harry had entered the pub.

As if he was more interested in the drivers' conversations on the table behind him.

Harry rejoined the table, but this time taking a seat that gave him a perfect view of the lone stranger.

KAT GRIPPED THE wheel tightly, concentrating, taking care not to get too close to the green van that bowled along just a hundred yards ahead.

DEADLY CARGO

She'd followed the vehicle south from Mydworth, through a couple of small villages, before it turned off the main road onto a winding, narrow lane that led up onto the downs.

And with the sun fading, that lane was deep in shadow now.

Kat reminded herself that people in this country drove roads like this every day.

How hard could it be?

Now, as she came onto a more substantial road, as it dipped and curved along this great range of windswept hills, with their view to the distant sea, she had to be careful not to be spotted in the van's rearview mirrors.

Early evening – not much traffic about. She didn't want to draw attention to the Alvis.

Without warning, the van suddenly veered off the main road down a farm track.

Too obvious if I follow, she knew.

Kat had no choice but to carry on driving, watching in frustration as the van disappeared over the meadowed hill and down into a valley.

She turned the Alvis around as soon as she could, then flew back to the junction and pulled in.

She pondered whether to turn the Alvis, drive down the track taken by the van. But much as she was tempted she knew it would be foolhardy.

She had faced decisions like this before, tailing someone late at night that the embassy wanted followed.

But here, now – no back-up, who knew how many people were down there? What if the van was somehow connected to the gang – and this was their base?

And with no trusty Colt to help…

No, best to retreat and come back with Harry tomorrow.

She looked around for some kind of landmark, so she'd know how to find the place again. Then she saw, lying on the grass, the tattered remnants of an old broken sign: *Brooke Farm*.

At least she now had a way of pinpointing the location on a map.

Time to head home, grab that bath, and then share notes with Harry.

Things were getting interesting. *And maybe... dangerous.*

*

HARRY DRAINED HIS pint, put it back on the table. *Time to go.*

The conversation had drifted from the robberies to soccer, racing, and the pros and cons of the new Austin engine.

He caught Drew's eye – one last question occurring to him.

"Before Fowler took over transport – who was in charge?" he said. "What happened to *them*?"

"You thinking maybe an old employee with a grudge?" said Drew.

"Possible."

"Hate to disappoint you," said Drew. "But old fella called Jones ran transport, nice bloke, fair he was. Had a heart attack – and that was that."

"Ah, I see," said Harry. "They got Fowler straight away then, did they?"

"Not exactly. White ran the schedules until Fowler started the next month. Or rather Miss Hollis did. I doubt White can tell a schedule from his own backside. All seemed to work okay."

Harry laughed. Drew's bitter opinions of management were getting predictable.

He stood up. "Well, thanks for your help. I do appreciate it."

"You're welcome," said Drew. "Reckon you've got a better chance finding these bastards than Timms."

"Even though I'm a toff," said Harry.

"Not your fault," said Drew. "You hold your pints, I can see. You're not as bad as some."

"Thank you! I'll take that as a compliment," said Harry, laughing. "Goodnight."

With a nod to the other men, he headed for the door and out into the gathering dusk.

Pulling his jacket close in the crisp evening air, he crossed the bridge over the river and walked up Station Road towards the town.

No street lamps down here and, apart from a thin sliver of moon, not much to light the way. To one side, lines of terraced cottages, dim lamps visible in some windows; to the other, trees and fields.

One day, maybe factories in those fields, thought Harry, aware of how much Mydworth was changing, and how *fast.*

A sound behind him interrupted his thoughts. Footsteps.

As ever, the instincts of so many years working in Intelligence abroad kicked in.

He turned casually as he walked, and spied a figure some fifty yards behind. Nothing unusual there *– but the figure – being noticed – stopped, and stepped into shadows.*

Harry carried on walking as if he'd noticed nothing and took a cut-through between the houses, a narrow alleyway that led to Old Lane.

Onto Old Lane, and a left turn to carry on walking up into Mydworth, houses on either side. These streets deathly quiet now, as ever on a weekday evening.

He crossed the road, again glancing casually down the road for a second.

There was the figure, a hundred yards behind, hugging the side of the lane, keeping to the shadows.

And Harry knew – no doubt about it – he was being followed.

He kept walking, up into Market Square, then right along the Arundel Road, this route making no sense, but for Harry a test, a way of confirming that his instinct was right.

But also a way to pull this unsuspecting tail into a trap.

Left now, off the Arundel Road and up School Lane, past the cricket pitch – every inch of this part of Mydworth so familiar to Harry – the figure still following.

And then another left down a dark alleyway with a zig-zag that looked like it might cut through to the High Street, but Harry knew was a dead end.

As soon as he turned, Harry sprinted to the zig-zag and crouched down by an old gate that backed onto the dairy.

He saw a shadow appear on the wall opposite – it paused, not moving, the man clearly wondering *did he come this way?*

The shadow moved, and Harry heard footsteps approaching, speeding up.

Harry tensed, took a deep breath, and then – as the figure passed just a yard from him – he uncoiled and leapt.

His shoulder caught the man squarely in the rib cage and he smashed him hard against the wall.

Harry's foot swung in to kick the man's feet right out from under him, so that the two of them fell together, Harry on the man's back, one hand reaching round to grab his arm and wrench it round, a *twist*, then pinning him, the other hand pressing the man's face into the dirt.

"Good evening. And who the *hell* are you?" said Harry, panting. The man didn't reply, so Harry bent his arm even further. An effective jolt of pain.

"Aghh, all right, all right!" said the man, trying to get up.

Harry spun the man round, so he was face up, but still pressed him to the ground.

And, well, maybe not a total surprise – it was the lone drinker from the pub.

"You were following me. Care to tell me why? Tell me, or I'm taking you straight to the police."

"I *am* the bloody police," said the man, spitting dirt from his mouth. "Get off me and I'll prove it."

"All right," said Harry. "No funny business, mind you."

And he stood, so the man could get up too. He waited while the man pulled his coat and jacket straight, then took out a small card from his top pocket.

Harry held it up in the faint moonlight to read.

The card looked like a police warrant card. The man's name, MacCulloch. But this card had one crucial difference, an address that few – unless they were in Harry's line of work – would know.

An address that concealed a very special identity. Not a police station but a branch of the British security services.

MI5. Domestic Intelligence.

"Cromwell Road," said Harry.

"That's right."

"Well, well. Very interesting. And how *is* Sir Vernon these days?"

"What?" said the man. "How the hell do you know—?"

Harry reached down and picked up the man's hat, dusted it down, and handed it to him.

"We're on the same side, MacCulloch old chap. Why don't we go and have a quiet nightcap in the King's Arms, and you can tell me exactly what you're doing in Mydworth... following me."

10.

CHECKING THE FACTS

BY THE TIME Harry finally got home to the Dower House, Kat had had her long bath, dressed, got the late supper all set, and had a cursory read through all the files that had been delivered from Excelsior.

One look at him and she could see that Harry felt as exhausted as she did.

All those pints probably didn't help either.

They sat together in the small dining room, sharing their stories of the day's events and steadily working their way through a bottle of Berry Brothers' claret.

"So, according to Mr MacCulloch, Reggie Drew's a card-carrying Communist, intent on fomenting revolution?" said Kat, after Harry had told her about the incident in the alley.

"And not just Drew," said Harry. "It seems our scientist friend, Arbuthnot, is a sympathiser too. Part of a radical group up in Cambridge."

"Gosh. Two of them in one factory. Better summon the nearest army battalion."

"Still though, don't you think... two of them... can't be a coincidence, can it?" said Harry. "Far as I could tell, Drew just wants to start up a union, but, you know, these chaps in Intelligence, they're always on the lookout for Bolshevists." Harry leaned forward. "They can run a tad paranoid."

Kat nodded. "But down here in Mydworth? I mean, what could he and Arbuthnot possibly be up to? Organising the dairy farmers?"

"The cows too, I imagine!"

They both laughed.

She watched Harry top up their glasses.

"Well, here's the thing, Kat. In the war, Excelsior *did* supply the army with radio kits. And – it's all a bit top secret, you know – but it seems they still have a contract with the War Office."

"So MI5 – and you – think that the robberies really might have a security connection?" said Kat.

"Not sure. But very possible," said Harry. "Which, coming full circle, makes your sighting of Arbuthnot even more important. Question is, who was driving that van?"

"Well – we know it wasn't Drew – you were knocking back pints with him."

"Only a couple."

"And some…"

"All in the line of duty, my dear."

"Clearly," said Kat, finishing her meal and sliding her plate away. "You think Fowler could be in league with Arbuthnot – stealing equipment? For some big Communist plot?"

"Does sound a tad unlikely, doesn't it? But still possible," said Harry. "However, how does that connect to the robberies? Or does it?"

"Right. Could be unconnected."

"Which wouldn't help us at all."

They both stood up, collected the plates and bowls, went into the kitchen.

"I tell you, this investigation has me going round in circles," said Kat.

"Me too. Especially tonight. Post pub, and all that."

"But Harry, one thing I do want to find out…"

"Go on."

"How come Fowler was so *useless* when he arrived at Excelsior – when his references were so excellent?"

"Good question," said Harry. "Right now, I think he's our top suspect – don't you?"

"Feels that way," said Kat. "Though we don't have a whiff of an idea who he might be working with. Okay then, let's make him our priority in the morning."

"Good idea. And also – we'll get the maps out, see what we can find out about Brooke Farm."

"Perhaps even head over there, do a little recce?" said Kat.

"Weather permitting? My idea of the perfect day out," said Harry. "Lovely walk, crawl through some fields and woods, then a quick break-in on a farm."

Kat looked at the pile of plates, then at Harry.

"Shall we just leave these – go straight to bed? I'm bushed."

"See you've had your bath. Allow me a quick shower, then I'll join you," said Harry.

Kat grinned at him. "You did hear me say 'bushed'?"

"Oh yes. No problems on *that* score."

And so they went to bed… somehow neither of them quite as tired as they'd thought.

*

Next morning, straight after breakfast, Harry made a bee-line for the phone, as Maggie came out of the kitchen, white apron on.

"Got to leave a bit early today, so I thought I'd get going on lunch…"

Kat saw Harry raise a finger. "Yes, operator, Winston 2475? If you would…"

He pulled the phone away from his mouth. "Maggie, whatever am I smelling? Fantastic, isn't it Kat?"

"Oh yes. Can we have lunch *now* please?"

Kat saw Maggie beam at that.

"Just a beef stew. Needs a few more hours. I'll make sure that when—"

But then Harry cleared his throat, and Kat spun away from Maggie to hear what her husband was up to.

"Yes, Mr Powell, why, yes we had an excellent tour. Some operation you have there. But my wife and I have a question."

Kat came closer, then leaned in so she might catch the voice of the owner of the factory.

Maggie scurried away, back to the kitchen, leaving them on the phone. And with Kat's face close to Harry's, he gave her a smile.

"Right, yes, Mr Powell – we do have some initial theories, if you will. But also, as I mentioned, a question or two."

Kat couldn't really make out Powell's words.

But no matter. She didn't move.

"Mr Fowler, you know the chap who handles your despatch department? We learned yesterday that he's a relatively new hire."

More squeaky words from the earpiece. Harry tilted it a bit so Kat could make out the answer.

Powell responded quickly. "Why yes, according to my son-in-law he was responsible for some excellent work for another company. Promised to revolutionise how Excelsior delivers its radios."

At that, Kat saw Harry give her an eyeroll. Perhaps thinking... *revolutionise by way of regularly scheduled highway robberies?*

"Right... and that company... don't suppose you know much about them?"

Again, the two of them sharing the earpiece, hearing Powell's answer.

"As I said, it's Edgar that handles this side of things. But I do believe it was the Tempt-Tea Biscuit Company. Big operation near Chichester."

"Biscuits, you say? Far cry from radios."

"Shipping is shipping, Sir Harry."

"Imagine so."

Kat leaned even closer, whispered to Harry.

"One more question just occurred to me. Don't suppose you've had any thefts from the factory itself? Stuff going missing?"

A pause. But not one, Kat thought, that suggested a man searching for the answer.

More of a cautionary *pause*.

With a nod of her head, she indicated to Harry to bring the earpiece even closer, their cheeks now touching.

She then thought of Edgar White's passion for technology and the future.

Maybe someday there will be a way for more than one person to properly talk and listen on a phone, she thought.

Still… she waited for the answer.

"Not as far as I know, Sir Harry. This something I should be aware of? You come across anything of that nature yesterday?"

"No, nothing in particular. Just a general question."

"By the way, Sir Harry, do you know about the travelling salesman problem?"

Harry's eyes went wide as he scanned Kat's face as if asking, *had she come across said problem before?*

Her hopefully blank expression indicated that, so far, she had not.

"You got a number of lorries, delivering to a number of locations… how does one find the fastest and – more importantly – the most economical way to make those multiple deliveries?"

Powell ended his explanation with an uptick in his voice indicating a question.

"And the answer is?" Harry said. His smile – Kat saw – showed that he knew he was being *cheeky*.

"Never been cracked! Still, the people who handle things like shipping routes, despatch, all that, still have to wrestle with it. And according to Edgar, this chap Fowler seemed to have some good ideas in that regard. Made total bloody good sense, with the roll out of our new Winchesters, to hire him."

Harry made a look as if to say, *do we have anything else to ask?* Kat shrugged.

So…

"Well then, Mr Powell. Thanks for this. We'll keep you posted, though I wouldn't expect any lightning breakthroughs. Least not yet."

Kat stepped away.

Harry slowly placed the phone down and turned to Kat.

"Well now. What in the world do we think about all *that?*"

MAGGIE HAD BROUGHT coffee out to the back garden.

A little chilly, but Harry would always opt to enjoy a morning coffee outdoors, save for extreme cold, rain or snow. None of those three today, so they enjoyed the steaming pot, while sitting on heavy wrought-iron chairs.

And appropriately enough, a plate of biscuits on the matching metal table.

He took one – a sugary shortbread.

"So, Lady Mortimer, you heard most of what Mr Powell said. A penny, and maybe a bit more, for your thoughts?"

Kat nodded. She was wearing a pair of khakis, a crisp blue shirt, a light scarf at her neck.

Certainly not glamorous, Harry thought. *And yet, with Kat? Absolutely smashing.*

"Think we do need to check out Fowler's history. Ace references – but terrible reputation? Chimes badly for me."

"Trip to the Tempt-Tea Biscuit Company?"

He saw Kat nod. "You agree?"

"Of course. Powell said it's near Chichester. Not a bad drive." He looked up at the sun. "Nice morning for it."

Harry leaned forward and took the coffee pot – poured them both a refill.

"Something else. With this scrutiny on Fowler…"

"Yes?" said Kat.

"Well, it looked to me like he was doing his level best to keep the routes secret, to actually *prevent* a robbery."

Kat nodded. "Which is exactly what you would do if you felt you might be suspected."

Harry smiled. "I do *so* like how your mind works, Lady M. And that triggers so many other questions to which we have no answer. All those radios. If they weren't stripped down – then where in my blue heaven did they go? I mean, police on the lookout. They'd notice, wouldn't they?"

"Back in my town? The NYPD? You bet they would."

"There – so that's another question for us to unravel."

"We haven't exactly unravelled any yet."

Harry laughed. "*That* we haven't."

"And Harry… what about Brooke Farm?"

"Yes. After our little trip to the biscuit factory?"

Kat smiled, and for a moment Harry thought… *wouldn't it be wonderful if they could defer all this…*

For other afternoon activities, right here in the Dower House.

But instead…

DEADLY CARGO

He stood up. "Let's get going then, and also perhaps you'd better tell Maggie to take that delicious stew off the stove. Might have to be our supper."

"Not sure she will like hearing *that*."

"True. But, I have to say, I think – in her eyes – you have become one of those people that can do no wrong."

Kat stood, laughing. "Then she doesn't know me well enough."

And with Harry gathering the plate and cups onto the tray, they walked back to the house.

With an unlikely visit to a biscuit factory next on their agenda.

11.

TRUTH AT THE TEMPT-TEA BISCUIT COMPANY

KAT WALKED WITH Wallace Bimble, the man who oversaw the noisy, humming factory that produced all the varieties of biscuits.

She found the place almost too much: the clatter and din of machines that mixed, rolled out and cut the dough; mixed with the sweet aroma from the baking cookies; to the conveyor belts that sped them to the packaging areas. Straight to a waiting army of women dressed more like army nurses, who would check, box and wrap, or seal in brightly-coloured tins.

"You seem quite busy," Kat said to Bimble.

Harry stayed back – close enough to listen, but with that unspoken shorthand they had developed. Kat took the lead.

Bimble had one of those moon faces, with eyes wide and round, matching oval spectacles and a toothy smile showing how much he enjoyed overseeing the factory's operation.

Worse things than being a man who brought cookies to all parts of the country.

Bimble stopped, face glowing as he answered. "*Busy* is not the word for it, Lady Mortimer. Hiring all the time."

"Looks like it's hard work."

Bimble nodded. "Indeed it is. Hard, but at a fair salary. We watch out for our own, you see. Always been the Tempt-Tea philosophy."

Kat nodded. This factory, despite the mayhem, seemed a happy place. Such a contrast to Excelsior.

She hurried to the question that had brought them there.

"As I said, Sir Harry and I are helping out a friend. And we have a couple of questions about a former employee."

Bimble nodded, his face losing a smidge of his eager glow.

"Yes?"

"Your former head of shipping. Mr Fowler?"

"Ah."

Now Bimble's glow faded completely.

"Apparently he did some excellent work for you?"

Kat felt Harry come closer to her side as Bimble scanned them both.

"If I might ask, you brought up his name because…?"

Kat took a breath. She didn't want to tell Bimble too much. Still…

"Mr Fowler, directly from leaving your company was hired to manage shipping for Excelsior Radios."

"So I heard."

"And, well, he was hired based on the reports of all the wonders he worked with your shipping department."

"Really? Self-reported wonders, that's for sure."

Bimble removed his glasses, looked down at the floor, as cookies of every variety dropped onto conveyor belts.

"Such reports would be – for lack of a better word, Lady Mortimer – 'untruths'."

In other words, Kat thought, *lies.*

"Fowler came in about a year ago from some place up north. Lot of bluster; but then he quickly antagonised our drivers, many of them long-term employees. Schedules all changed. Basically, he took what was more or less working and made a proper hash of it."

That prompted Harry: "And you didn't reveal this to Excelsior?"

"Of course I did!"

Kat glanced at Harry, then back to Bimble.

"I'm sorry, Mr Bimble, you mean you put that information in Mr Fowler's references?"

"Too right I did," said Bimble. "Would have been highly irresponsible not to!"

"Do you remember who you wrote to?"

"Oh yes. Mr White. Mr Edgar White."

Kat thought back to the excellent references she'd seen in Fowler's file.

What was going on here?

"Can I ask you, how you remember his name so well?"

"Ah well, there was some confusion at the time. Mr White's letters somehow got delayed, and I wasn't able to complete the references until some weeks after Fowler left us here."

"You mean, Excelsior gave him the job without checking his references?"

"I gather they were in a hurry. They must have decided to risk it. We are, after all, a highly regarded company, Lady Mortimer. And with our business booming, I expect your Mr White took that as evidence of Fowler's competency. I imagine they felt they could take it on trust not to have hired a... a... wrong'un like Fowler."

A wrong'un, thought Kat. It certainly sounded that way. Had Fowler forged his references to get the job at Excelsior? Somehow intercepted and destroyed the real ones?

"But he was?" Kat asked.

"A wrong'un? Oh yes."

Kat waited a moment. "Mr Bimble, were there any other worrying things about Mr Fowler?"

She caught Harry giving her a look, as in, *good one.*

Bimble seemed to be distracted by his whirring domain of biscuits and tins, before returning his owl-eyed gaze to the two of them.

"You know, it's not really my place to, well, gossip about an ex-employee."

Harry quickly added an extra nudge.

"Whatever you say will remain completely between us. Just trying to help a fellow business owner, suffering through a rather bad patch. I'm sure you can sympathise."

At this, Bimble said, rather straight-faced, "I can't imagine what I would do if someone stole a lorry filled with my Tempt-Tea biscuits! I'd be absolutely devastated, I tell you!"

Kat nodded – the man was in earnest.

"But – all right, *entre nous* and all that – it was commonly known that Fowler liked to gamble," continued Bimble. "The races, not that I've ever been. Word was, it put a big dent in his finances."

"Gambling? Interesting," Kat said. "Anything else?"

Now Bimble looked even more uncomfortable – if that was possible.

"Well. There is *something else*. We couldn't really prove it. Rumours, really, but it appears that if you wanted a *timely* delivery, then all it required was a few extra pounds passed Fowler's way," Bimble added. "And *that* is detestable."

"I agree," said Kat.

She looked over at Harry, the two of them now armed with a rather more complete picture of Fowler.

Liar. Gambler. Crook.

And suddenly the Excelsior robberies seemed to have their prime suspect.

And yet... why did Fowler make a show of trying to keep the drivers' schedules secret?

Whatever is going on, there's a lot more to be uncovered, thought Kat.

But for now, she extended her hand.

"Thank you, Mr Bimble. I must try your *coo*— biscuits very soon."

"Oh, yes, Lady Mortimer, Sir Harry. I'll have a tin sent over to your home straight away."

"Too kind," Harry said, also shaking the man's hand.

Kat turned and, with a smile, said, "Think we can find our way out. And thank you again. This has been… quite important."

AND ONCE OUTSIDE, the late afternoon air so refreshing after the sugary sweet cloud inside the factory, Kat turned to her husband.

"So, what say you, Harry?"

"As you said, *interesting*. But how does it fit together? If Fowler is involved…"

"Which would seem very likely."

"Yes, but is he in it alone? How does the operation work? And the big question we still haven't answered – where have all those radio phonographs disappeared to?"

"Where indeed."

"So then… okay. I think it's time to check out Brooke Farm, don't you?"

"Yes," she said. "But maybe better after sunset?"

"Night time for spying? Always a good thing."

"Then maybe – in the interim – we drop by the WVS, give Nicola the good news about Barry Hobbs?"

"Cup of tea while we await darkness?"

"You and your tea."

"And later, if we've been good and successful amateur detectives…"

"Home for cocktails and Maggie's stew!"

Kat grinned.

As she got into the driver's seat, finally having gotten over the habit of going to the left side of the vehicle to drive, she thought, *Are we finally getting closer to the truth?*

12.

THE SECRET OF BROOKE FARM

ENGINE AND LIGHTS off, Harry coasted the Alvis down the grassy track, and parked well away from the deep-maroon barnlike structure just ahead.

It looked just like any other innocent farm building.

To one side stood the ruin of what must have been the original Brooke Farm: roof fallen in, ivy winding through the abandoned stone shell.

Next to the barn, he could see the green van that – Kat had told him – had carried boxes of who-knows-what out of the Excelsior factory.

If the van was back again tonight, he felt sure there must be somebody in the barn.

But from the outside, all looked quiet.

Gently he opened the car door, climbed out, and took stock, listening for any sounds of movement.

"All set?" he whispered, as Kat hopped out of the car and stood beside him.

"You know, Harry – this part of what we do? Love it."

He looked at her, her face catching a splash of light from the crescent moon. "Me too. Takes me right back to sneaking up to some shady address in the back streets of Cairo."

She nodded. "Or, in my case, Istanbul. Like being a kid again."

"Though tonight – with this gang – think it's no kids' game we're playing."

And now, they crouched low and moved, staying tight to a row of sycamores and scattered bushes, getting closer to what seemed like the one entrance into the barn.

A large sliding door, probably designed to accommodate a herd of cattle coming home after a day of sleepy ruminating.

The door thick enough so they heard no sounds from inside.

Revealing not a clue of what might be going on.

"OKAY," WHISPERED HARRY. "Going to give it a yank. I'd say on 'three' we dash in. Element of surprise and all. Not sure just how easy this barn door will be to open."

"Ready when you are," Kat said.

He gave her a quick smile. "Oh, I know *that*. Now…"

He turned back to the door, the large metal handle grasped with two hands, leveraging his body to provide as much *oomph* to his tug as possible.

Then he pulled…

And, surprisingly, the heavy massive barn door just *slid* open, as if someone had attached slick new rubber wheels for the door to roll on, gliding open almost too quickly, Harry teetering off to the side.

Kat fired out a hand to catch his arm.

And when they turned back to the open door and peered in, they saw concrete steps ahead. And beyond the steps, deeper in the building, obscured by boxes and stacks of crates, a strange, pulsing glow.

Harry shot Kat a look, as if to say, *hope no one heard our little break-in…*

And they climbed the steps and walked through the stacks of boxes towards that glow, hearing voices, two men. Were they about to finally meet the man who'd driven Arbuthnot here the day before with all those crates?

And perhaps find out… *what is this all about?*

KAT STAYED CLOSE to Harry, step for step, catching glimpses of the two men at the far end of the barn who seemed so absorbed that they didn't notice that they were no longer alone.

But closer now, hearing those voices more clearly, she thought she recognised that second voice.

Edgar White.

What was he doing here?

With just a few more steps she finally got a clear view of the area that was bathed in such bright light.

It looked like some kind of improvised workshop. Giant electric lights hung above workbenches arranged in a U shape, strange electrical equipment and machines filled the room, and there were rows and rows of switches and dials and flickering lights.

The place reminded her of the crazed laboratory in that movie *Metropolis* that she and Harry had seen in the Regent Street Cinema on their last trip to London.

She saw White standing with his back to her in front of something on a tripod, Arbuthnot just steps away on one side, half-hidden behind a large metal table.

And on that table stood a device that supported a dinner-sized metal plate that was rapidly spinning.

"Yes, yes——" Arbuthnot said, his voice quite squeaky with excitement.

And as he spoke, something happened that stunned Kat.

Because on that spinning plate, she suddenly could see the *image* of Edgar White even as he gestured from yards away, with his hands.

White's moving image appearing somehow on that spinning plate!

And Kat thought... *it's not a mirror, not a movie, not a reflection.*

The device was actually capturing what White did, and displaying it across the room!

She looked at Harry, and his eyes showed that same mix of astonishment and confusion.

He mouthed a word.

"Ready?"

A nod from Kat.

Harry stepped forward and in a quite civilised tone – considering the science-fiction setting – spoke the words, "Good evening gentlemen."

ARBUTHNOT SPUN AROUND, his glee melting like an ice cream in July.

White moved away from the platform he had been standing on, and turned towards Harry and Kat.

She didn't feel any threat – at least not yet – but clearly the two men were not at all happy with their unannounced arrival.

"What the hell are you two doing here?" said White, looking from one to the other.

"Guess we might ask the same question of you," said Kat quietly. "I mean, sneaking equipment out of the Excelsior factory late at night, driving to this deserted old barn?"

White paused, his eyes still darting from Harry then back to her.

"Actually, that's *none* of your business. Mr Arbuthnot and I are merely..."

Kat saw him glance across at Arbuthnot as if he might have an excuse already prepared. But Arbuthnot simply stood, his hands hanging limply, his eyes bulging with alarm.

"Let me hazard a wild guess," said Kat. "Merely setting up an extremely elaborate and expensive laboratory, to do things that your father-in-law knows absolutely nothing about?"

White had no answer.

And she watched as Harry walked over to the platform where White had been standing.

"Tell you what *I'd* really like to know," said Harry. "What is this… *thing* that we just saw? Not a movie of some sort, now is it?"

White looked again at the scientist at his elbow and actually gulped. While she and Harry didn't know what the secret of this place was, they knew at least it was – in fact – a *secret*.

White cleared his throat.

"All right then. I'll tell you. And I just hope you don't destroy all our work, not to mention the company's future, with your careless meddling."

Harry responded. "Yes, to meddling, but I do take umbrage at the word 'careless'. Either way, Lady Mortimer and I are all ears."

White nodded.

He turned back to the metal table with the disc sitting atop a series of boxes with glowing lights, tubes, and wires snaking everywhere.

"*This* – Sir Harry, Lady Mortimer – is the future."

HARRY TRIED TO follow as White, aided by technical details from Arbuthnot, explained what they were looking at.

"Some people are calling it *tele*-vision. It is, quite simply, if you will, radio with images. And not *just* images but motion and sound. Broadcast through the air."

"Radio with movies?" Kat said.

"No. Not exactly. See, well, in its current form it can transmit – just like radio – live sound and *live* images. Early days of course. You saw my image. Tad wavy, breaks up a bit…"

"I'm working on that," Arbuthnot interjected defensively. "It's all to do with the quality of the oscillators, you see and the frequen—"

"Yes, yes. A lot of issues to resolve. But this, even at this stage, puts Excelsior ahead of any other company in England. Maybe even the world!"

Arbuthnot again added, "You see, there's Baird, and also the Americans, that fellow Farnsworth, he's very—"

White stopped that morsel of information about competitors with a quick swivel of his head to the scientist, then back to Kat.

"Well, there you are. But you have met my father-in-law. He thinks the company begins and ends with radio phonographs! He just doesn't understand – this is going to kill radio! He can't see the future. No vision at all! But if we don't pursue the research and development of this, well, within a few years Excelsior will be left in the dust."

Arbuthnot nodded at that.

Before Harry asked his next question, he had an important thought. *This is all very interesting – but does it help with the investigation?*

"So Mr Powell, the man who actually owns the company, knows nothing about this?" A nod from White. "Knows nothing about the resources… the money being siphoned off to support it?"

This time, another gulp accompanied the nod.

"Who else knows about this place?" said Harry. "This research?"

"Nobody," said White, a tad too quickly for Harry's liking.

"Really?"

He saw White's eyes flick across to Arbuthnot again, as if hoping to be let off the hook.

For the first time since he and Kat had started on this case, he had a sense of one or two jigsaw pieces coming together.

Maybe there was a connection to the robberies after all.

"You're not telling me that Fowler doesn't know what you're up to? He must have seen this equipment being smuggled out of the factory."

White didn't answer.

"Fowler forged his references, didn't he?" said Harry. "And *you* were told. And yet – you turned a blind eye…"

White looked away.

"Can you explain that?" Harry prodded.

White turned back. "Okay. Sure. Fowler, always snooping around. Discovered what me and Arbuthnot were up to. Threatened to tell all to Powell. Unless I kept my mouth shut about the forged references."

"Blackmail," Kat said.

"That what it's called?" White said. "I had no choice."

"I see," said Harry. "Well, I'm pretty sure it's not our business to expose this. And I must say, I for one think you may be onto something here. Might be crucial to Excelsior."

"Precisely!"

"But still, we *are* investigating. Not sure we can avoid eventually mentioning this."

"God, no."

"Hang on though. I do have an idea. In exchange for a *favour*."

Now Harry felt Kat's eyes on him.

How he loved it when he caught her interest as well.

Though – knowing Kat – she might already have had the same idea.

"Some time, I'm not sure when, you need to have Mr Powell come see this."

"He'll positively *explode*. He'll fire me."

"His daughter's husband? Unlikely. Show him this wonder. Make your case, man. You promise to do that and I see no need to mention what Lady Mortimer and I have found out here on Brooke Farm."

"All right," said Edgar. "I agree."

He looked at Arbuthnot who didn't seem so sure. "*We* agree."

"But we will still need a favour," said Harry. "We've been getting nowhere tracking down how these robberies happen."

White nodded. Kat's eyes on him still, a small smile on her lips. *Oh yes,* he thought, *she's on the same page.*

"So, I'm thinking, with no hard evidence, it's time to set a *trap.*"

"A trap?"

"Yes. To draw out whoever – within Excelsior – is providing this gang with its Intelligence. And, tit-for-tat as they say, we'll need your cooperation in setting said trap."

For a few seconds everything was still in the stage-like setting of the laboratory. Only the hum of the machines and the strange rhythmic pulse of light from Arbuthnot's contraption.

Until White, whose secret involved images magically floating through the air versus radios mysteriously disappearing from lorries, broke that silence.

"I'll do it," he said.

13.

THE TRAP IS PLANNED

KAT WATCHED AS Harry walked around the laboratory.

"Now, I don't exactly have all the details worked out. I'm sure," he looked right at Kat, "my wife may have some important elements to add. But basically, it's this…"

She watched as Harry had let his hand casually touch the top of the seemingly magical disc.

"Oh, please do *not* touch that," said Arbuthnot. "It's a specially designed, ultra light—"

"Oh, so sorry. Amazing thing. Anyway… Kat do let me know your thoughts."

She smiled. "Oh, I will."

"What might induce our robbers to hit a specific delivery?"

White shrugged. "I don't know. Shipments are pretty much the same, a broad mix of models, going here, there to different shops, distributors."

But Kat immediately saw where her husband was headed.

"What if a shipment wasn't… *pretty much the same?*"

"What do you mean?" White said.

She walked closer to her husband.

A look to him to make sure she indeed had grasped his idea.

"You must be a mind reader, Kat. This barn is *full* of magical things tonight."

"Makes sense, no?" she said. "How about a truck filled only with the top-of-the-range model – the Westminsters? As many as can fit in the vehicle."

"Exactly," Harry said. "You see, Mr White, what if we make it a completely irresistible target? Worth three or four of their other hits. They'd have to go after it."

White shook his head. "But we have no such shipments scheduled."

White may be an excited proponent of the future, but in this setting, hatching a trap? A tad dim, Kat thought.

"I think what my husband is suggesting, is that you *create* such a shipment."

"With *actual* Westminsters?"

"Of course! The prize has to be real."

"B-but couldn't the robbers – even if they knew – decide *not* to go for it? For some reason."

Kat saw Harry fire her a look, as if admitting… *all carefully planned traps have their Achilles' heel.*

"Well, yes. Might happen. Though I still think it's a shot worth taking."

Now White looked at Arbuthnot as if the so far uninvolved scientist might have an opinion. However, the man remained mute.

"B-but why do you need me?" White said.

"You can set that shipment up. Overnight, I imagine."

"Well, I can. Though it would require Mr Powell's approval. But the robbers – how do we make sure they learn of it?"

"Well," Kat said, "Here's the thing, Mr White. Sir Harry and I have really narrowed things down to one person. One suspect."

"And that person is…?" asked White.

Kat took a breath. "Fowler."

"I see," said White.

"Dodgy past, short of money…"

"Has a fondness for the horses too, apparently," Harry added.

"And of course," said Kat, "every shipment that leaves the factory goes through his office. The routes. Last-minute changes. What the loads are. Right?"

"Absolutely. But you really think he's our man?" said White. "I'd have put my money on one of the drivers."

"Fowler's already broken the law, just getting his job," said Harry. "And he's been blackmailing you. Hardly a solid character reference."

Kat continued, "All you have to do, is set the shipment up. Make sure Fowler knows the route, what's in the load – and that it's got to be hush-hush. And, if nothing happens, then hey – it might even clear him."

"Let's hope *that* doesn't happen!" Harry said.

White nodded, seeing the plan and his role.

"When do we do this?"

"Sooner the better," Harry added. "Tomorrow, late afternoon? A run to Manchester."

"It's very short notice. I don't know what driver we'd have available, and anyway, what does the driver do if he is stopped? I mean – it's putting someone deliberately in harm's—"

Kat saw Harry put up a hand.

Her brain hadn't raced far enough ahead of her husband for the next bit.

"No worries about the driver. None at all."

Now Kat joined White and the scientist at looking at Harry.

"*I'll* drive."

KAT WALKED RIGHT up to her husband. "You'll drive? A big truck loaded with radios?"

"Oh, I've done some of that in my various posts. Like driving a car, only bigger you see."

"And when they stop you, steal the radios, what then—?"

Harry's smile faded.

"Well, I shall have my trusty Colt at hand, and—"

But Kat had already started shaking her head,

"No. Too dangerous. Bunch of thugs, greedy, armed with shotguns, and you with a little pistol."

"I'm rather good with that little pistol."

"You know, you had me on board with this 'trap' till, well, just now. Of course, if there was a way that I could follow right behind you, get the police involved as well…"

"I'm sure our friendly band of radio robbers would spot a tail from miles away."

"Some other way," Kat said. "There must be."

Which is when Arbuthnot sniffed and said, almost with a boyish sense of pride.

"Well – I do believe there is!"

"THIS IS A WIRELESS set we're developing for the War Office."

Arbuthnot had led everyone over to another table.

On it, a small canvas khaki satchel.

Arbuthnot unbuckled the straps and took out a small wooden box, with headphones and a microphone attached.

"A portable wireless set, actually. About as compact as you can get…"

"Amazing," Harry said, inspecting it. "We had portable sets back in '17 but nothing like this."

"I *know*," said the young scientist, beaming. "Knocks Marconi into a tin hat, doesn't it?"

He watched as Arbuthnot slid the radio back into the satchel and slipped the shoulder strap over one shoulder.

"And look how easy it is to carry."

Harry looked at Kat, beginning to understand the role this wireless radio could play in the great scheme of things.

"You see, this set's compact enough to fit under the passenger seat. No one will spot it."

And though Harry recognised that Arbuthnot was some kind of technological genius, apparently, he had other skills as well.

"You get stopped. Maybe they don't knock you out. No reason to, really. Then, when they are about to leave…"

"Right. I get it. Jump in the back of their lorry with this and, er, do what exactly?"

"You broadcast to us, over here."

Arbuthnot walked to another table where a similar contraption sat, but this one had a loudspeaker and a large dashboard with dials and knobs.

"We'll be able to hear you loud and clear."

Harry turned to Kat, wondering what she thought about where this was headed.

"There you go, Kat. I can let you know where we're going, with a compass and all that. And when we stop, I just peep out, look for a sign, a landmark, and you bring the police along straight away. Easy!"

He saw Kat scratch her chin. Had she turned a corner on the plan?

"Okay. Might just work. Course, I'll be right here."

"Of course."

"Let the local police know ahead of time."

"Yes, right. Get Sergeant Timms and company on full alert."

"Still, Harry… dangerous."

He paused at that. This was not the time for an easy lie.

"True enough. But you and me… we've faced plenty of danger before. All turned out tickety-boo, didn't it?"

"Tickety…? Only needs one time for it *not* to."

Harry wasn't sure what he would do or say if Kat balked at the whole idea.

But then she shrugged.

"Okay," she said. "A lot to get in motion before tomorrow night. You need practice with the equipment. We need to get word to Fowler. Mr White here needs to alert Mr Powell's office. Think urgency will help."

"Absolutely," said Harry. "I do love urgency."

She walked closer to the radio dashboard. "And I need to understand this as well."

Arbuthnot's face wrinkled as if unsure. But then he nodded.

Harry took a breath.

Less than twenty-four hours to get the trap ready.

And everything depends, he thought, *on Fowler taking the bait.*

14.

A TRAP IS SPRUNG

HARRY SAT ON the wooden bench at the bus stop, watching the early evening traffic heading in and out of Mydworth half a mile away.

Surprising how busy it gets, he thought. *And these days hardly a horse and cart to be seen.*

He looked down at the wireless radio in its satchel on the seat next to him. He'd spent half the day practising with it, while Kat was on the receiving end of his messages.

That part had all gone okay, and Mr Powell had approved the plan, ensuring that all the dummy orders and invoices as a "priority" shipment were prepared and sent down to Fowler's office.

Powell's reaction to the possible target of the trap? "If it's him, I shall personally strangle the *bastard*."

And Harry was pretty sure that the owner of Excelsior meant it.

Key to making this whole thing work, was that this shipment shouldn't arouse suspicion as anything more than a last-minute *urgent delivery*.

To this end, Harry had persuaded White that they needed the help of Reggie Drew – and although White was suspicious of the union organiser, he understood that this plan wouldn't work without him.

Harry wondered how the chaps at MI5 would feel about his enlisting a "dangerous Bolshevist" to the cause.

He and Kat hadn't taken long to decide that Arbuthnot and Drew were not conspiring together to pass secrets to the Communists.

As it turned out, Drew was more than glad to help, and asked no questions after Harry offered a perfunctory explanation.

And now Harry was here, kitted out in drivers' overalls, waiting for Drew to turn up in the six-wheeler lorry and hand over the shipment to him.

He checked his watch.

Five o'clock. He stood up and peered down the road towards Mydworth.

And sure enough, there was the Excelsior lorry, bang on time, heading up the gentle hill out of town, its gears grinding.

He watched the lorry pull in at the bus stop, and Drew jumped down and came round the front of the cab to Harry.

"Here she is," said Drew. "Full tank of fuel – not that you'll be needing it from the sound of things."

"Thanks for the reminder," said Harry.

He saw Drew give Harry's driver's outfit the once over.

"Not bad," said Drew. "You'd never guess—"

"That I'm a toff?"

Drew laughed.

"That the radio?" he said, pointing at the satchel.

Harry nodded. Drew opened the passenger door of the cab, and both of them stashed it securely under the passenger seat, Drew covering it with an old dustsheet.

"Sure I can't come along with you?" said Drew.

"Appreciate the offer," said Harry. "Do indeed. But the whole plan depends on them overpowering me, and something tells me you wouldn't let them do that."

He watched Drew laugh.

"You're not wrong there," he said.

They shook hands.

"I appreciate the help."

"Anything that stops my lads getting hit on the head," said Drew, "and then getting the blame for it."

Harry nodded, then walked round the cab and climbed into the driver's seat. He turned the ignition, grabbed the large black steering wheel. And as soon as there was a gap in the traffic he pulled away.

Drew's lone figure at the bus stop getting smaller in the wing mirror, as he headed towards Petersfield and the north.

KAT SAT WITH Edgar White at the large wireless set.

"I imagine we may have quite a wait, Lady Mortimer."

Kat nodded. "Could be a wait for nothing if the robbers don't take the bait."

She took a breath. In front of her, lights and flickering tubes, and at the centre a large dial.

Arbuthnot was there with the air of a proud father showing off his offspring.

"All set to the right frequency."

She turned to the man and smiled. "Great. Now, since we may have a few hours, don't suppose we could rustle up a pot of coffee?"

The looks on their faces showed that request was a bridge too far.

"Tea perhaps?"

"Sure."

Smiles as White nodded, and hurried off to the side of the building.

Arbuthnot, again with his odd demeanour, said, "Actually, we have biscuits too."

Kat nodded.

Will wonders never cease? she thought.

HARRY QUICKLY NOTED that driving this machine was not *quite* as easy as the small army lorry he had driven back in '17 when the situation had called for it.

The thing was big, sluggish, and with a gear box that seemed to groan in protest every time he shifted up or down.

He even muttered to the machine, in his defence, "I *am* using the clutch, damn it."

But after a while he found the giant steering wheel began to feel quite comfortable, and he learned that, though the fully loaded lorry was slow to respond, it did eventually take instruction.

And at least the roads were wide and well-paved. Like all the deliveries that Excelsior did these past few months, his route stuck entirely to main roads.

Of course, if someone tried to divert him, then that would be different story.

In the west, the sky had turned a rich purple. The lorry's lights were already on. Night was falling.

And while Harry found this all rather exciting, part of him also thought it was *rather intimidating to be the cheese in the trap.*

No one had been killed in any of the robberies.

So far.

WHILE KAT SAT and sipped her perfectly hot cup of tea – no milk, spot of sugar – she noticed that Arbuthnot had drifted away, over to where his amazing device sat. Tinkering with it, while White looked on.

The two of them – lost. Not just to the vision of creating the complicated machine, but also to a vision of the *future.* Kat could hardly imagine people having such devices actually in their home.

She turned back to the console which was glowing bright and totally quiet.

This waiting was hard.

ONE HOUR ROLLED along, then another, but Harry knew from his interviews that the robberies never occurred at a set time during the run.

He imagined that was part of the gang's system to make things as unpredictable as possible, but also as the traffic got lighter, to make the robberies easier to stage.

Besides the satchel with the wireless radio below the seat next to him, he had tucked his Colt under his seat, ready for a quick grab.

And while he drove, he began to think of the way things might play out.

He had been outnumbered before – that was no novelty.

Still, *this* was different.

And at least one of the possible outcomes of this night didn't end well for him.

But he shook off that possibility.

I'll face things when I face them.

THEN – JUST AHEAD he saw another lorry.

Not the one described by the other drivers, but something larger, with a canvas cover to protect the cargo.

The lorry was stopped, at an angle, blocking the way forward.

"Well, well," Harry said to himself.

I may have just got lucky.

Of course, it could be another driver in distress. Far away from the nearest Royal Automobile Club telephone box for roadside assistance?

No matter – he'd have to stop.

He downshifted, the lorry's gearbox roaring in protest as he braked, slowed and stopped.

To see, *no one at or near the truck.*

"Well, that's interesting."

But then – in one of the wing mirrors – headlights.

And from the height and spacing of the lights, it looked like another lorry pulling up tight behind him.

Harry's left hand reached down to feel for his revolver, out of its holster.

But that lorry had raced fast, nearly hitting Harry in the rear, a screech of the brakes on the tarmac road, and even as Harry felt the cold metal of the gun, suddenly he heard a sharp *crack* on the driver's side window.

Harry turned to see a man standing on the lorry's running board.

The man had his own gun – only his was pointed at Harry's head.

He waved the muzzle to signal that Harry should lower the window… which he did.

The voice.

"You will follow that lorry. I'll be behind. Understand?"

Now the question was reinforced with the gun muzzle planted squarely and hard on Harry's temple.

Harry thought of half a dozen ways he might remove the weapon from the man.

But *that* wasn't the plan. Instead, making what he hoped was his best *"I'm really terrified"* face, Harry nodded.

Another man slipped into the lorry beside him, also with a gun.

The man at Harry's window grinned.

"Do what I say, and you won't be hurt."

That accent. Heard it before somewhere.

Question is, where?

EDGAR WHITE WANDERED over to where Kat sat, this waiting both tedious and terrible.

"Doing all right, m'lady?"

The "m'lady" sounded odd in this futuristic laboratory on an abandoned farm where they hoped to use an experimental wireless radio to capture armed robbers with a taste for luxury radios.

She made a small smile.

"Maybe nothing will happen."

White nodded.

"Either way," Kat said, "we'll know soon enough."

She looked over at Arbuthnot. "At least your scientist there seems to be making good use of the time."

White grinned. "Don't think Arbuthnot ever sleeps."

HARRY FOLLOWED THE other lorry down a narrow lane. A perfect spot for them to unload the Westminsters, and peel away.

In the wing mirror, he could see that the lorry behind had more men next to the driver, so they had a group of at least five to pull off the heist.

When they finally turned off the lane into a field and stopped, he looked at the man beside him, careful to stay "in character".

"Lovely spot. Been here before?"

But the man said nothing, unless you counted the threatening daggers that emanated from his eyes.

"Apparently not," Harry said.

So far, the course of the robbery had matched the other drivers' descriptions. Everyone quiet.

No talking, save for the one man, who now opened the door to the Excelsior lorry and snapped, "Get down. Sit on the ground in front of your lorry. Hands behind your head."

Harry nodded as he got out, knowing he was leaving both his gun and his wireless set behind.

The man pushed him down to the ground hard. When Harry's hands didn't immediately go to the back of his head, fingers intertwined, the man said, as if it might be a capital offence, "Hands *behind* your head and keep them there!"

And then Harry suddenly identified the man's accent.

So distinctive.

French, and in this case, quite specifically, in tone and roughness, the *patois* one stumbled upon in the more interesting *quartiers* of Marseilles.

As if all the Louis XIV niceties had been leeched out of the mother tongue.

So was that why the robberies were all conducted in silence? Not because the men feared being recognised – no.

But because they were *French*?

Was the man giving the orders the only one who had passable English?

Harry now sat, hands locked behind his head, as both the canvas-backed lorry and the white panelled one backed up to the Excelsior lorry.

And the unloading began.

The crates with the giant radios transferred so swiftly, and strapped down tight.

A massive payday – ten thousand pounds at least – and being done so efficiently.

These boys knew their trade.

But Harry also wondered, would they just leave him here? Abandoned like all the other drivers, to skulk back to the factory with an empty lorry?

Or with a payday this big, might they have other ideas?

Either way, Harry knew he'd soon find out.

15

THE END OF THE ROAD

FINALLY – IT WAS done.

Once again Harry's new friend walked over to where he lay on the ground, and gave Harry an unnecessary kick to get his attention.

"You do *not* move. For thirty minutes."

Harry nodded, but then couldn't resist. "All right," he said, in his best driver's voice. "Trouble is… my hands tied up like this… how'm I supposed to see my wristwatch, eh?"

That only brought another kick to Harry's ribs, before the man walked away.

As Harry turned back to look down the dark deserted lane, behind him the fully loaded lorries were ready to go.

Well, it's now or never, Harry thought.

He imagined that the robbers would assume that – like all the other drivers – Harry would remain in place for a good while, frozen with fear.

Yes – there *was* a smidge of fear in the air.

But he rolled over onto his front and began crawling, slowly as possible, until he came abreast of the driver's side door of the Excelsior lorry.

The lorries ahead, lights on, engines running, ready to go.

Harry watched.

Waited.

He had done his fair share of sprinting and cross-country runs back in the day.

But what was called for now would be nothing more than amazing.

Amazing, that is, if he pulled it off.

"I CAN'T STAND this," said Kat to the console.

White, seated next to her, nodded.

This waiting… all too much.

And she knew that whatever was happening with Harry, this… just sitting here…

Was far worse.

ONLY SECONDS LEFT now, surely, and Harry rose up, clasped the abandoned lorry's door handle, popped it open.

Just enough for him to lean in, yank the satchel out – maybe a bit too roughly – and also grab his Colt, slide it under his belt.

Then – he reached down to his calf. Strapped in its sheath, his old Flying Corps knife.

The one thing a pilot swore by if ever things turned bad, in the air, or on the ground.

Now – he just had to pray that it was dark enough, no one scanning those rearview mirrors – he raced to the back of the canvas-covered lorry, used the knife to tear a jagged, long slash.

The lorry began to pull away just as Harry finished.

As gently as he could, he tossed in the wireless radio.

And, almost losing his grip on a back strut of the lorry, he pulled himself in – rolling into the back where the full load of crates allowed him little room to move.

But he was in the lorry, the vehicle already picking up speed, fields flashing by through the slash in the canvas, the light from the headlights reflected on trees.

He reached into his pocket, and flipped out his old compass.

Hard to see in the lorry's dark interior, but he could just make out the key coordinates, the dial luminous: N, S, E, W.

He looked down at the satchel that had been treated – he knew – a little roughly for the precision instrument inside.

He pulled out the radio set that he had practised with for most of the day.

KAT STOOD UP. She just couldn't sit anymore.

Then…

"Hello, Harry here. I say, anyone getting this?"

She flew back to the seat in a flash, as White and Arbuthnot also hurried over.

Kat grasped the microphone like it was part of Harry's body and she'd never let it go.

"Harry, are you *okay*?"

"Never better. Though these chaps, they do like to play rough. Okay, I'm in one of the lorries."

"More than one?"

"Guess they wanted to make sure they got all the goods. Heading almost due south. Not sure at all what road. But they stopped me near Swindon. So start tracking. Doing maybe forty… forty-five miles an hour."

Kat turned to a nearby table, still holding the microphone.

"Okay. Got your position roughly. Any idea where they are headed?"

"None at all! But wherever they're going, I am too. Will keep you posted as we merrily roll along."

"Harry – take care of yourself."

"Always."

She looked at White, but then – *what the hell.*

"I love you."

"I should hope so. You know, one way or the other, we *will* get to the bottom of this."

"Don't like the 'one way or other' part."

"Just stay with me, Kat. We'll be okay."

Kat looked at the map: a coin representing – more or less – where she thought the van might be.

"We'd better be."

AN HOUR ROLLED by, Harry checking the compass constantly, updating Kat, amazed that the radio was still working.

But then he felt the lorry slowing down.

He took off the headphones, squeezed between the stacked crates, risked sticking his head out, seeing houses, streets...

Back to the radio, headset on.

"Kat – on the map, got any idea what town I might be passing through? Biggish place, heard a railway for sure."

"Harry – could be Andover?"

"Okay. Don't think we're stopping here. What's ahead?"

"Well, as the crow flies, due south, I'd say... Portsmouth."

"*Portsmouth.* If that's where we're headed, I'll recognise it. Even at night. Makes sense too."

"Why?"

"Place is a *maze*. Docks, streets, cars, lorries. Ships loading and unloading from here, there, everywhere."

"You think you're heading for a ship?"

He laughed at that. "Can't be certain – but I guess we'll know soon enough."

ANOTHER HOUR LATER, and Harry felt the lorry slowing again, crunching down through the gears as it went downhill – a long, slow hill.

He knew this road of old – making a slow descent down to the busy city of Portsmouth.

And the smell of the sea, mixed with the diesel and smoke of the city, and – even at this late hour – the sound of traffic and people and pubs, just confirmed that.

He felt the truck sway as it navigated the narrow, twisting streets, the noises from the docks getting closer until they came to a stop.

A brief conversation, then the heavy clank of gates opening, and the lorry lurched forward.

Into the docks – it had to be.

Finally, the lorry slowed and he heard the engine being turned off.

Again, he sneaked through the crates – peered out through the slashed hole at the back of the lorry.

An eerie darkness – just pools of light from tall dock lights in a dank sea mist that swirled across a bleak expanse of concrete quay.

He pressed his face tight to the canvas to look in the other direction. He could see the shape of a small freighter, her deck lights visible.

He ducked back in, to the wireless set.

"It's Portsmouth all right. Stopped beside some kind of freighter, can't see the name. Think we're in the old port, make sense, not too close to the naval base. Get hold of Timms, have the locals here alerted. Tell them to get moving. This lot moves *fast*."

DEADLY CARGO

"Will do."

"Jolly good. Should be easy enough to round these chaps up. Anyway, I'd best hop out before they start unloading and find a stowaway. Think this is bye for now, Kat."

Harry reached down and pushed the wireless set to the side, checked that his gun was still in place.

And with that done, he hurried to slip out of the back of the lorry, hoping to vanish amidst the crates and vehicles near the freighter.

But someone was already there.

The man from Marseilles, who now used his gun to whip Harry across the face, sending him crashing to the stone dock.

Then – *blackness*.

KAT TURNED TO White and his scientist – both with their eyes locked on her.

"Any idea where the nearest telephone might be?" she said.

White shrugged. "No idea,' he said. "Probably Mydworth."

Kat frowned. Every second was vital. She looked back at Arbuthnot – and the radio.

"That thing – can you contact the police on it?"

Edgar White stepped forward. "Lady Mortimer, I'm really not sure whether that's a good—"

But Arbuthnot intervened, almost brushing his boss to one side.

"Can't talk to the police *direct*," he said. "But we have the military frequencies – we can use one of their channels, ask them to—"

"Do it," she said. "Use Sir Harry's name – it *always* works wonders for me. Alert Timms, the Portsmouth police and anyone you can think of. And if they want to talk to me, tell them I've gone."

"Gone?" said White. "Gone where?"

"To Portsmouth."

The two men looked at each other as if such a trip, miles across country, and still in darkness, by an American no less, was total…

Madness.

But Kat was already racing out.

Ready to see just how fast their Alvis could go.

16.

SILENCING THE WITNESS

WHEN HARRY CAME to, he realised he was lying on the hard stone of the quay by the side of the lorry.

Turning his head slowly – it throbbed with pain – he saw that nearly all the radios had been off-loaded to the dock, and even now were being hauled into the freighter.

Just a few crates left.

He must have been out for some time.

He tried to get to his feet, but his hands were tied and he tumbled back to the ground.

He looked up.

The man who'd clipped him on the head stood over him, his gun pointed at Harry. And Harry's own Colt now tucked in his belt.

"You're not a lorry driver."

"How on *earth* did you guess? Actually, I don't think I played the role *too* badly."

The humour, Harry noted, was lost on the man.

He glanced across at the freighter, the tattered name on its hull visible in the foggy light: *Le Marais*.

These radios were bound for the continent, most likely this man's home town, or maybe Calais, or anywhere where the port authorities didn't ask too many questions.

Then, dispersed for a small fortune in cash throughout Europe.

Which is why they never appeared for sale here.

And as he looked, Harry realised something.

They can't let me live.

And the reason they hadn't already shot him?

These docks, even late at night, were still too busy. Too many people nearby. Gunshots in a naval port would cause an alarm.

So, Harry wondered, *what was their plan?*

"Stand up," the man muttered.

"*Bien sûr*," Harry said.

Letting the guy know that he had begun putting things together. Even though that wouldn't improve the odds of him staying alive. With difficulty, Harry stood.

"Turn around. Walk."

And when Harry turned, he saw that he faced the end of the quay. The solution to these robbers' problems became clear.

Walk me out there, hands tied behind my back, maybe tie my feet, then watch me bob my way to death by drowning.

Not the cleanest of murders. But then with a heist this big, these men could go back to France, and disappear.

And when he thought… France… it sparked a memory, but that thought was quickly lost as he felt a punch in the ribs and the man pushed him forward.

"Walk, I said!"

HARRY REACHED THE edge of the dock, the dark murky water below – the twinkling lights of Gosport visible across the harbour through the wraiths of mist.

He turned to face the man. The gun was aimed at him.

"Say, how about we turn around and talk this over somewhere away from here?"

The man spat the next words out as if there something personal between him and his captive.

DEADLY CARGO

"You can jump, or I will *push* you. And then – that is it."

And though Harry imagined he might be able to float a short while, with his legs free, it wouldn't be long before he'd lose that battle, and sink under the chilly waters of the Solent.

And perhaps, he thought, my new friend here might aid the process by kicking at him as he tried to remain afloat.

The freighter would leave before the police turned up. And that would be that.

And while Harry felt an icy vein of fear running through him, he tried to buy as much time as he could.

"You know, I really do swim a lot better with my hands untied, and all. Perhaps you wouldn't mind…"

But that only triggered the man to close the distance between himself and Harry, clearly intending to use the gun – not to shoot – but to jab in to Harry's midsection, and send him flying backwards.

So much for buying time.

The man only steps away…

When Harry heard another voice. A female voice.

Oh so welcome.

And familiar.

"Stop right there, or you're a dead man."

KAT HELD HER own revolver, also a souvenir kept from her time working for the US government abroad; not standard issue at all, but after a few tricky encounters in more than one European capital, reluctantly granted to her.

She watched as the man stopped, turned – his pistol now aimed at her.

Harry meanwhile stood poised at the edge of the dock, but not yet in the water.

The man's eyes were the only things that really caught any light, his gaunt cheeks covered in a dark, dusky stubble.

But then he slowly turned and looked up to the ship moored so close by.

"You see... my men. Guns too, you stupid—"

"Oh, I wouldn't say *that*," said Harry. "Lady Mortimer is known to frown on any such pejorative remarks... especially when uttered by someone who is *actually* stupid."

Kat wondered, *Is this a distraction? Or dangerous?*

But the man who now had Kat in his sights said, "One person, one gun. But up there, *all* those guns are aimed at you."

And while Kat didn't hazard a look, she knew that what the man was saying was probably true.

She'd get a shot or two off but then be cut down herself.

Her mind raced, searching for a solution.

Harry, right at the dock edge, shouted, his voice carrying loudly. "I should warn you."

What's he doing? thought Kat.

"Yes, you win in the guns department, certainly," he continued. "But see my Kat here? She's actually, a *crack* shot. Never misses – least not that I ever saw. So whatever happens here – after *her* shot – I'm afraid you won't be around to witness a thing."

Kat grinned. If nothing else, what Harry said was *completely true*. And it was giving the gunman something to think about.

"Put down the gun," the man said. "Now."

Kat's answer: a slight extension of her arm, signalling a steady determination to fire back.

The seconds ticked by.

A breeze off the water, carrying with it the smell of the sea, tinged with oil from all the ships that came in and out of this harbour. Until...

DEADLY CARGO

A noise.

Incongruous.

Ridiculous, Kat thought.

Bells jangling like Christmas gone mad, but then accompanied by the unmistakable roar of four, no, five cars racing across the broad expanse of the dock, lights flashing.

The police.

She kept her gun steady. The man's eyes shifted, knowing that, tables turned, his options were just about up.

In seconds, the police were there, car doors flying open, constables tumbling out, some of them guns in hand. She saw Timms but also others, most of whom she guessed had to be locals, Portsmouth police, rousted from bed.

Surrounding the whole scene.

And only then, did she lower her gun, as the man who had been about to kill her husband did the same thing.

And she walked to Harry.

HARRY WAITED, FEELING like he was taking the first normal breath in a few minutes.

"However did you get here so fast? Ahead of the local constabulary?"

Kat had gone to his back, quickly undoing the simple knot in the rope that tied his hands together.

"Soon as I knew where you were headed, I took off. Figured minutes might count."

"Oh, didn't they just. Was blacked out for a while. Nasty knock to the head. A bit of tardiness and you'd be in the market for a new baronet!"

His hands untied, Kat came to his front. And suddenly gave him a kiss. "Don't you ever say that."

But then Harry saw Timms, and a few of the other police surrounding the man from Marseilles, handcuffs appearing, other police already on the freighter.

This could have turned into a pitched battle.

"Come on," he said to Kat.

And Harry walked over to the man who had held him captive.

The boss.

But for Harry... not the chap they were really after.

Time to find out if Fowler was really the man on the inside.

"Sergeant Timms – if you don't mind. Lady Mortimer and I would like a quick word with the gentleman here. Before you haul him off. Oh, and I do believe that's my Colt you have there."

Timms handed Harry his gun back, then Harry spun the man around so he faced both himself and Kat.

"Now then, I'm sure you don't want this all pinned on you, right? Things will go easier for you if you just give us the name of your contact in Excelsior?"

The man's eyes darted from Harry to Kat, and back again.

His mouth moved as if whatever he was about to say was so difficult.

But then he spat at the ground – and shook his head.

His face defiant.

Harry turned to Kat, who shrugged.

He gave Timms a nod, and two constables stepped forward, led the Frenchman away.

"Sir Harry, sir," said Timms, turning to them both. "My constable back at Mydworth has Mr Fowler in custody at the station. Mr White explained the situation, sir."

"Good man, Timms," said Harry. "Why don't we see you back there in a couple of hours? Have a little chat with him?"

"Strike while the iron's hot, sir!" said Timms, then he turned to join the other police rounding up the gang.

Harry took Kat's hand and they both walked over to the Alvis, where Harry saw a familiar figure leaning against the side of the car, pipe in hand.

And on the ground next to his feet – the radio set.

"If it isn't Mr MacCulloch," said Harry.

"Sir Harry," said the MI5 man, tipping his hat. "Lady Mortimer, pleasure to meet you."

"Delighted, I'm sure," said Kat.

"Reassuring to know Cromwell Road has my wellbeing in mind," said Harry.

"Oh, I wouldn't exactly say that," said MacCulloch. He lifted up the satchel. "Truth is – we can't have experimental War Office equipment going astray."

Harry smiled. But then Kat stepped forward.

"Clearly you know that Mr Arbuthnot and Mr Drew helped us out, then?" she said.

"Aye."

"So I trust you'll be taking them both off surveillance."

"I shall make a note in their files," said MacCulloch, his face set.

"They're honest working men," said Kat, and Harry could sense she wasn't going to leave this alone.

"That's as maybe," said the MI5 agent, and Harry thought he wasn't going to budge.

But then, he seemed to soften.

"Tell you what," he said. "Until now, we've not had a field trial of this little contraption. So, Sir Harry, you write up a little *interdepartmental* report for us, and I'll see what I can do for your pals in Mydworth."

With another tip of his hat, MacCulloch hoisted the satchel over his shoulder and headed over to Timms and the police cars.

Harry watched him go then turned to Kat.

"Well – that's something, at least," he said.

"We'll see," said Kat.

They both watched the police convoy drive away, the Frenchman handcuffed in the back seat of Timms's car.

"Could have done with a full confession there," said Harry, shaking his head, disappointed. "Trap half-sprung."

"Guess we just have to hope Fowler cracks," said Kat.

"Want me to drive?" he said.

"After a bump on the head?" said Kat.

"Feel quite spiffing."

"I'm sure you do," said Kat. "Nevertheless – *I'm* driving."

Harry settled in the passenger seat – in truth, gratefully – as she started up and they headed back to Mydworth. But he couldn't totally relax.

What if Fowler wriggles out of this? he thought.

17.

A LATE-NIGHT CHAT

"ALL RIGHT," SAID Fowler, leaning back in his chair, arms folded, "I'll 'fess up to the dodgy references. Fair enough, shouldn't have done that, you caught me fair and square."

Fowler looked away, acting – Kat thought – about as uncomfortable as a man could.

He went on: "Sure, I twisted Mr White round my little finger over his dodgy enterprise up at the farm, though Sergeant Timms here is going to find it hard to trump up some charge to cover that. But I'm telling you there is no way in God's little heaven I'm going to let you take me down for the robberies. *I – didn't – do it!*"

Kat stared at Fowler across the small interview room table, looking for any sign that he was spinning a line.

And not seeing one.

She turned to look at Harry.

He raised an eyebrow briefly – a sign she knew well, meaning "we're not getting anywhere here".

In the corner, she could see Sergeant Timms clearly wanting to put this interview to bed, already an unusually late hour for the small Mydworth police force.

She turned back to Fowler.

"Okay. Fair enough," she said. "Why don't we continue this in the morning, if Sergeant Timms is happy to include us?"

"As you wish, m'lady," said Timms. "Can't say Mrs Timms would disagree with you, seeing as it's nearly midnight."

Kat stood up, and she and Harry went out of the holding cell and into Timms's office, then out onto the steps for some fresh air.

Even though she and Harry had showered and eaten back at the house, she still felt totally exhausted.

"Call it a day?" said Harry, clearly registering her mood. "Can't win 'em all, Kat."

"Guess so. I just feel – I don't know – like he's holding out on us somehow."

"Start again tomorrow? Fresh minds."

Kat nodded.

"One thing I don't buy. He says he got away with the fake references because White would do anything to stop his father-in-law finding out about the secret laboratory."

"That's right."

"And you believe him?"

"Hmm, well, I have to admit it does sound a little rum. Hardly a hanging offence spending a little off-books, as it were."

"What if he had something more serious on our friend Mr White?"

"Could be."

"If only one of the crew on that boat would squeal. If not, are we back at square one? What if we were totally wrong? What if it is Drew after all? Or one of the other drivers?"

Kat looked out at the line of rooftops – a sliver of moon painting the tiles a milky white.

"You know that thing you do, when you're interviewing someone?" she said, turning back to Harry. "That 'think back, tiniest detail' thing?"

"I do indeed."

"Well?"

"Oh, you mean me?"

"Yes. The robbery. What happened. What you remember. The detail."

"Well, I do remember that chap didn't hold back when he walloped me."

"Ouch, I know. You can have a nice whisky for that when we get home."

"Thank you, doctor," said Harry, smiling. "Okay, memory time…"

Kat waited while he did what she'd asked.

"Wait a minute," he said, suddenly gripping her shoulders, his face lighting up. "There *is* something!"

"Go on."

"It didn't happen today. Dammit, why didn't I remember this? Both Drew and Barry Hobbs told us, but we didn't follow up on it."

"But Harry – what? Tell me!"

"Ha, come on, you'll have to wait and see. We're going back in there before dear old Timms shuts up shop. I've got one very big question for our friend Mr Fowler! And I think we're about to learn the real truth about the blackmail."

And with that, he spun round and, with her hand in his, they went back into the police station.

HARRY WATCHED WHILE Kat knocked on the door of the tidy cottage, with its tall trees surrounding it, a well-tended garden, and neat gravel path.

All soon to be abandoned.

But perhaps not the way the owner planned.

The house, dark – no surprise at this hour. Above them, that moon now high over the town, casting its soft spell.

Nothing for a moment from inside. Another flurry of hard raps, and a light switched on. Steps.

The door opened.

And he saw Mary Hollis, dressing gown on, pulled tight, startled at the late-night intrusion.

"Sir Harry, Lady Mortimer... what on earth are you doing here?"

Kat, taking a step forward, said, "Mary... I think you already know that."

THE WOMAN HAD backed up.

And Kat quickly told her how the planned robbery went down this night, all the men arrested.

And also, who they said had supplied the information on the lorry to the gang, its route, its cargo.

And despite Mary Hollis shaking her head, Kat knew the woman wouldn't be able to maintain that façade for long. All the evidence needed would eventually be found: the money Mary got, the property purchased in France, her arrangement with the experienced mob in Marseilles.

But Kat had one great question: "Why? Why did you do it, Mary?"

The woman stood frozen, as if she might continue the sham of denying her role. But then – and Kat felt as if there was a bit of trust in this – she answered the question.

"DURING THE WAR, I handled so much. Had so much responsibility. Moving those medical supplies, getting field hospitals up and running. People's lives were entrusted to my care, *my* judgement. And then at Excelsior, when I took over despatch for those months, everything worked so *well*."

Kat nodded. She noted Harry being quiet. Listening.

"And yet," Mary said, then more softly, "when the time came to make that job permanent, was it offered to me? No. Old Powell couldn't imagine giving it to a mere *woman*."

Kat nodded. "I understand. Not fair, right?"

"Yes, you do get it, don't you?"

"Seen it myself."

"Then I thought, well, if I was going to be passed over, shoved to the side, kept as a mere secretary, I could make a different life for myself."

"In France?"

"Yes. Leave the company stuck with that fool Fowler. And Edgar White."

"You had an affair with him, yes?" said Kat.

And Mary's eyes went wide at that.

"I did," said Mary. "I *thought* he was different. But he was never going to leave his wife. I could see that. And I could sense some people in the factory knew."

"So you ended it?"

"It's about self-respect," said Mary, looking right at Kat.

As if Kat could understand.

And she did.

But Kat also knew that now, it was time.

For the cat to come out of the bag.

"So then, after *all* that, you took a holiday in France, made some enquiries, arranged to have the radios stolen, shipped to the continent…?"

And Kat saw Mary Hollis actually smile.

"Got me, eh? Yes. Smart, no? All the paperwork at Excelsior came through my office. I typed the orders, made out the invoices, processed the requisitions."

"Even today," said Harry. "Mr Powell confirmed on the telephone he passed the secret order across your desk."

"And you two didn't even suspect the woman in the office, did you?" said Mary, shaking her head at Harry.

"All this time," said Kat, "you were watching the chaos. Counting the days till your getaway?"

"Don't you see, Lady Mortimer?" said Mary. "What wonderful payback. I imagine, even you could do the same thing?"

And in the dim light of the woman's parlour, Kat shook her head.

"No. There are unfair things. Done to women. By men. I *know*. But you think what you did changes that? That's not the way the world will change."

Mary's face fell, as if she had hoped she could convince Kat.

Harry walked over. Slowly. Speaking gently.

"Mary. The police, Sergeant Timms, Constable Thomas... they're outside. Gave us this bit of time. And you, to get dressed, gather some things..."

The woman looked from Harry to Kat.

"I don't suppose this could be done in the morning? It's so late and—"

Harry shook his head. "I'm afraid not. But take your time. We'll stay here. Walk you out."

The woman nodded. Kat thought she seemed close to tears, her planned life abroad...

Just vanished.

Before Mary Hollis turned to go upstairs and get dressed, she gazed at Kat and said, almost incongruously or maybe simply appreciating the understanding, "Thank you."

And then she walked up the stairs, to begin her future, now so suddenly changed.

WHEN HARRY FINALLY drove them back to the Dower House, he started turning on the house lights as if it was supper time.

Kat hung her light jacket in the hall closet.

"Harry. What on *earth* are you doing?"

"A day like today surely calls for a cocktail before bed, don't you think?"

"Oh yes," Kat said, walking over to one of the floor lamps that Harry had turned on.

Switching it off.

"Mix away. But I think maybe we can enjoy whatever concoction you create upstairs?"

"Cocktails in the bedroom? *Do* like the way you think, Lady Mortimer."

Kat laughed. "I know you do, Sir Harry. And I will see you up there."

And as she walked up the stairs, both of them safe in the Dower House, Kat felt like this house, their home, was a sanctuary amid everything they had faced today.

I am really *beginning to love our life in England,* she thought.

And she also felt fortunate. Aware of the women – in this town, in this country – for whom the cards hadn't fallen so favourably.

NEXT IN THE SERIES:

DANGER IN THE AIR

MYDWORTH MYSTERIES #6

Matthew Costello & Neil Richards

The famous aviatrix Amelia Earhart has come to England on a mission to raise Money for her planned continent-spanning air rally – with all-female pilots.

Lady Lavinia naturally supports the amazing Amelia, inviting her to stay at Mydworth Manor. But when Amelia's life is threatened - Harry and Kat must figure out who is behind this deadly game before it turns fatal...

ABOUT THE AUTHORS

Co-authors Neil Richards (based in the UK) and Matthew Costello (based in the US), have been writing together since the mid-90s, creating innovative television, games and best-selling books. Together, they have worked on major projects for the BBC, PBS, Disney Channel, Sony, ABC, Eidos, and Nintendo to name but a few.

Their transatlantic collaboration led to the globally best-selling mystery series, *Cherringham*, which has also been a top-seller as audiobooks read by Neil Dudgeon.

Mydworth Mysteries is their brand new series, set in 1929 Sussex, England, which takes readers back to a world where solving crimes was more difficult — but also sometimes a lot more fun.

Lightning Source UK Ltd.
Milton Keynes UK
UKHW011602040121
376396UK00005B/1363